BLOW

50 Cent
and
K'wan

POCKET BOOKS, a division of Simon & Schuster, Inc
1230 Avenue of the Americas, New York, NY 10020

First G-Unit/MTV/Pocket Books trade paperback edition July 2007

For information about special discounts for bulk purchases, please contact Simon & Schuster Special Sales at 1–800–456–6798 or business@simonandschuster.com.

Manufactured in the United States of America

10 9 8 7 6 5 4 3 2 1

ISBN-13: 978-1-4165-4060-1
ISBN-10:   1-4165-4060-1

Dedicated to T.S.C.
(The Too Smooth Crew)
Tony Council
Tyrone Council
Albert Javier
Ramon Pequero
Michael Wilson

Let these words serve not only to expose the Judases,
who have gladly eaten from our plate only to serve
us poison apples in return, but to let you know
that right or wrong, you are still in my thoughts.
They say that the lady of justice is blind, but I'm
about to give that bitch some glasses.

—K'wan

"The game is not for the faint of heart,
and if you choose to play it,
you better damn well understand the rules."

Prince sat in the stiff wooden chair totally numb. The tailored Armani suit he had been so proud of when he dropped two grand on it now felt like a straitjacket. He spared a glance at his lawyer who was going over his notes with a worried expression on his face. The young black man had fought the good fight, but in the end it would be in God's hands.

He tried to keep from looking over his shoulder, but he couldn't help it. There was no sign of Sticks, which didn't surprise him. For killing a police officer they were surely going to give him the needle, if he even survived being captured. The police had dragged the river but never found a body. Everyone thought Sticks was dead, but Stone said otherwise. Sticks was his twin, and he would know better than anyone else if he was gone. Prince hoped that Stone was right and wished his friend well wherever fate carried him.

Marisol sat two rows behind him, with Mommy at her side looking every bit of the concerned grandmother. It was hard to believe that she was the embodiment of death, cloaked in kindness. This was the first time he had seen Mommy since his incarceration, but Marisol had been there every day for the seven weeks the trial had gone on. She tried to stay strong for her man, but he could tell that the ordeal was breaking her down. Cano had sent word through her that he would be taken care of, but Prince didn't want to be taken care of; he wanted to be free.

Keisha sat in the last row, quietly sobbing. She had raised the most hell when the bulls hit, even managing to get herself tossed into jail for obstruction of justice. She had always been a down bitch, and he respected her for it.

Assembled in the courtroom were many faces. Some were friends, but most were people from the neighborhood that just came to be nosey. No matter their motive the sheer number would look good on his part in the eyes of the jury, at least that was what his lawyer had told him. The way the trial seemed to be going, he seriously doubted it at that point.

Lined up to his left were his longtime friends, Daddy-O and Stone. Daddy-O's face was solemn. His dress shirt was pinned up at the shoulder covering the stump where his left arm used to be. It was just one more debt that he owed Diego that he'd never be able to collect on. Stone smirked at a doodling he had done on his legal pad. Prince wasn't sure if he didn't understand the charges they were facing or just didn't care. Knowing Stone, it was probably the latter. He had long ago resigned himself to the fact that he was born into the game and would die in it.

Prince wanted to break down every time he thought how his run as a boss had ended. To see men that you had grown to love like family take the stand and try to snatch your life to save their own was a feeling that he wouldn't wish on anyone. *No man above the team* was the vow that they had all taken, but in the end only a few kept to it. To the rest, they were just words. They had laughed, cried, smoked weed, and got pussy together, but when the time came to stand like men they laid down like bitches. These men had been like his brothers, but that was before the money came into the picture.

CHAPTER 1

6 months earlier

"**C**ome on Daddy-O, you know me." The young man reminded him, not believing that he'd been turned down. He could already feel the sweat trickling down his back and didn't know how much longer he could hold out.

Daddy-O popped a handful of sunflower seeds in his mouth. He expertly extracted the seed using only his tongue and let the shells tumble around in his mouth until he could feel the salty bite. "My dude, why are you even talking to me about this; holla at my young boy," he nodded at Danny.

"Daddy, you know how this little nigga is; he wouldn't let his mama go for a short, so you know I ain't getting a play."

"Get yo money right and we won't have a problem," Danny told him, and went back to watching the block.

"Listen," the young man turned back to Daddy-O. A thin film of sweat had begun to form on his nose. "All I got is ten dollars on me, but I need at least two to get me to the social security building in the morning. Do me this solid, and I swear I'll get you right when my check comes through."

Daddy-O looked over at Danny, who was giving the kid the once-over. He was short and thin with braids that snaked down the back of his neck. Danny had one of those funny faces. It was kind of like he looked old, but young at the same time . . . if that makes sense.

There was a time when Danny seemed like he had a bright future ahead of him. Though he wasn't the smartest of their little unit, he was a natural at sports. Danny played basketball for Cardinal Hayes High School and was one of the better players on the team. His jump shot needed a little fine-tuning, but he had a mean handle. Danny was notorious for embarrassing his opponents with his wicked crossover. Sports was supposed to be Danny's ticket out, but as most naïve young men did, he chose Hell over Heaven.

For as talented as Danny was physically, he was borderline retarded mentally. Of course not in a literal sense, but his actions made him the most dimwitted of the crew. While his school chums were content to play the roll of gangstas and watch the game from afar, Danny had to be in the thick of it. It was his fascination with the game that caused him to drop out of school in his senior year to pursue his dreams of being a *real nigga*, or a real nigga's sidekick. Danny was a yes-man to the boss, and under the boss is where he would earn his stripes. He didn't really have the heart of a soldier, but he was connected to some stand-up dudes, which provided him with a veil of protection. The hood knew that if you fucked with Danny, you'd have to fuck with his team.

"Give it to him, D," Daddy-O finally said.

Danny looked like he wanted to say something, but a stern look from Daddy-O hushed him. Dipping his hand into the back of his pants, Danny fished around until he found what he was looking for. Grumbling, he handed the young man a small bag of crack.

The young man examined the bag and saw that it was mostly flake and powder. "Man, this ain't nothing but some shake."

"Beggars can't be choosers; take that shit and bounce," Danny spat.

"Yo, shorty you be on some bullshit," the young man said to Danny. There was a hint of anger in his voice, but he knew better than to get stupid. "One day you're gonna have to come from behind Prince and Daddy-O's skirts and handle your own business."

"Go ahead wit that shit, man," Daddy-O said, cracking another seed.

"No disrespect to you, Daddy-O, but shorty got a big mouth. He be coming at niggaz sideways, and it's only on the strength of y'all that nobody ain't rocked him yet."

"Yo, go head wit all that *rocking* shit, niggaz know where

I be," Danny said, trying to sound confident. In all truthfulness, he was nervous. He loved the rush of being in the hood with Daddy-O and the team, but didn't care for the bullshit that came with it. Anybody who's ever spent a day on the streets knows that the law of the land more often than not is violence. If you weren't ready to defend your claim, then you needed to be in the house watching UPN.

The young man's eyes burned into Danny's. "Imma see you later," he said, never taking his eyes off Danny as he backed away.

"I'll be right here," Danny said confidently. His voice was deep and stern, but his legs felt like spaghetti. If the kid had rushed him, Danny would have had no idea what to do. He would fight if forced, but it wasn't his first course of action. Only when the kid had disappeared down the path did he finally force himself to relax.

"Punk-ass nigga," Danny said, like he was 'bout that.

"Yo, why you always acting up?" Daddy-O asked.

"What you mean, son?" Danny replied, as if he hadn't just clowned the dude.

"Every time I turn around your ass is in some shit, and that ain't what's up."

Danny sucked his teeth. "Yo, son was trying to stunt on me, B. You know I can't have niggaz coming at my head that way."

"Coming at your head?" Daddy-O raised his eyebrow. "Nigga, he was short two dollars!"

"I'm saying . . ."

"Don't say nothing," Daddy-O cut him off. "We out here trying to get a dollar and you still on your schoolyard bullshit. You need to respect these streets if you gonna get money in them," Daddy-O stormed off leaving Danny there to ponder what he had said.

■

The intense heat from the night before had spilled over to join with the morning sun and punish anyone who didn't have air conditioning, which amounted to damn near the whole hood being outside. That morning the projects were a kaleidoscope of activity. People were drinking, having water fights, and just trying to sit as still as they could in the heat. Grills were set up in front of several buildings, sending smoke signals to the hungry inhabitants.

Daddy-O bopped across the courtyard between 875 and 865. He nodded to a few heads as he passed them, but didn't really stop to chat. It was too damn hot, and being a combination of fat and black made you a target for the sun's taunting rays. A girl wearing boy shorts and a tank-top sat on the bench enjoying an ice-cream cone. She peeked at Daddy-O from behind her pink sunglasses and drew the tip of her tongue across the top of the ice cream.

"Umm, hmm," Daddy-O grumbled, rubbing his large belly. In the way of being attractive, Daddy-O wasn't much to look at. He was a five-eight brute with gorilla-like arms and a jaw that looked to be carved from stone. Cornrows snaked back over his large head and stopped just behind his ears. Though some joked that he had a face that only a mother could love, Daddy-O had swagger. His gear was always up, and he was swift with the gift of gab, earning him points with the ladies.

Everybody in the hood knew Daddy-O. He had lived in the Frederick Douglass Houses for over twelve years at that point. He and his mother had moved there when he was seven years old. Daddy-O had lived a number of places in his life, but no place ever felt like Douglass.

Daddy-O was about to head down the stairs toward 845 when he heard his name being called. He slowed, but didn't stop walking as he turned around. Shambling from 875 in his direction was a crackhead that they all knew as Shakes. She tried to strut in her faded high-heeled shoes, but it ended up as more of a walk-stumble. She was dressed in a black leotard that looked like it was crushing her small breasts. Shakes had been a'ight back in her day, but she didn't get the memo that losing eighty pounds and most of your front teeth killed your sex appeal.

"Daddy-O, let me holla at you for a minute," she half slurred. Shakes's eyes were wide and constantly scanning as if she was expecting someone to jump out on her. She stepped next to Daddy-O and whispered in his ear, "You holding?"

"You know better than that, ma. Go see my little man in the building," he said, in a pleasant tone. Most of the dealers in the neighborhood saw the crackheads as being something less than human and treated them as such, but not Daddy-O. Having watched his older brother and several of his other relatives succumb to one drug or another, Daddy-O understood it better than most. Cocaine and heroin were the elite of their line. Boy and Girl, as they were sometimes called, were God and Goddess to those foolish enough to be enticed by their lies. They had had the highest addiction rate, and the most cases of relapses. Daddy-O had learned early that a well-known crackhead could be more valuable to you than a member of your team, if you knew how to use them.

"A'ight, baby, that's what it is," she turned to walk away and almost lost her balance. In true crackhead form, she righted herself and tried to strut even harder. "You need to call a sista sometime," she called over her shoulder.

Daddy-O shook his head. There wasn't a damn thing he could call Shakes but what she was, a corpse that didn't know it was dead yet. Daddy-O continued down the stairs and past the small playground. A group of kids were dancing around in the elephant-shaped sprinkler tossing water on each other. One of them ran up on Daddy-O with a half-filled bowl, but a quick threat of an ass whipping sent the kid back to douse one of his friends with the water. Stopping to exchange greetings with a Puerto Rican girl he knew, Daddy-O disappeared inside the bowels of 845.

■

The first thing Daddy-O smelled when he stepped off the elevator was piff. Weed itself had a distinct smell, but piff was more like scorched honey. No matter how many windows you opened or how much air freshener you sprayed, if you had a good grade of haze, you couldn't hide it. Piff, haze, Barney, purp . . . whatever you chose to call it, was up there as far as top-shelf weed went. It wasn't as good as official Cali-Chronic or some of the other high-end grades of weed, but far more accessible.

Daddy-O tapped softly on the door and waited. There was a shuffling of feet and the clink of the peephole as someone tried to peek through it. After getting confirmation from someone, the bolts began to slide free. The rush of smoke that hit Daddy-O in the face was enough to make him dizzy. The entire house reeked of weed and cigarettes. Daddy-O stepped inside the house with the door slamming behind him.

The young man who had opened the door for Daddy-O was tall and beanpole thin. He wore his hair in cornrows that were pressed against his head beneath his do-rag. When he smiled at Daddy-O, his sharp cheekbones threatened to pierce the skin. Daddy-O had known Sticks for a while, but he still hadn't gotten used to his cadaverous appearance.

The coffee table in the middle of the living room was littered with ashtrays and loose PS2 games. Stone, who was Sticks's fraternal twin, sat on a milk crate tapping away on a joystick. He glanced once at Daddy-O then went back to his game. His opponent was a brown-skinned kid who Daddy-O only knew as Knox.

Knox was a little older than the rest of them, but still hung around with the young boys when it was convenient. He had a boxed head with beady eyes that seemed to be looking everywhere at once. Knox didn't have an affiliation with any crew in particular; he just clung to whoever was holding it down. It wasn't unusual to see Knox making moves with different cats in and around the projects. As long as he stayed out of Diego's way he was cool. Much like E, Knox had managed to get on Diego's personal shit list. No one was quite sure what he did to get there, but it was common knowledge that Diego didn't like him. Whenever he would catch Knox trying to make a move, he would have Manny run him off the block. Everything Knox did had to be done in secret, and that probably explained why he was always skulking around in the shadows. Since Knox had come home from a skid bid, he had taken to spending time with E. Birds of a feather, Daddy-O reasoned. Knox had never done anything to him personally, but he knew that wherever you saw Knox you were more than likely to see E. Daddy-O stepped all the way into the apartment and, as sure as hell was hot, the devil sat at the wooden table against the wall.

CHAPTER 2

Killa-E sat with his back to Daddy-O, facing the kitchen where there was another man standing over the stove. E was a pale Puerto Rican kid who wore his hair in a buzz cut that never seemed to grow beyond a certain point. He had a tender jaw and a long pointed nose that made you wonder if white wasn't somewhere in his genetic makeup. He cast his red-rimmed eyes behind him to Daddy-O and smiled. Though the smile was innocent enough, Daddy-O knew that E was more than he appeared to be.

"What's good," E said, extending his hand.

"Sup," Daddy-O said, giving him a fist-pound. He knew E through Prince, and though Prince seemed to trust him, there was something about E that never sat right with Daddy-O. Prince said that Daddy-O had never gotten over the fact that E fucked his high school sweetheart, but Daddy-O never admitted to it.

"What's good, daddy?" the man standing over the stove smiled at Daddy-O. He was tall, but not too much more than average. His mahogany skin had taken on a milk chocolate glow from the summer temperature and the added heat from the stove. In one hand he clutched a coffee pot with contents that had begun to turn a milky white, while a cigarette burned in the other.

"What it is, Prince," Daddy-O raised his fist in the air.

"Trying to get this cookie right for E," Prince said, lifting the pot to eye level so he could examine the rice-cake-shaped object at the bottom of it. "I'll be finished in a minute, but in the meantime why don't you twist that bag of five-six on the table."

"Fo sho," Daddy-O said, sliding into the chair closest to the kitchen and Prince. He began breaking the weed up on a CD case trying not to think on how much E's presence was offending him. He cut his eyes up from his task and found E looking at him. It wasn't a malicious look, but a curious one. E knew that Daddy-O didn't like him, and he had an idea why, but he didn't know for sure. E got off on being able to read people and therefore play to their egos, but it didn't work with Daddy-O and it irked him.

E had lived in the projects longer than Daddy-O, but didn't have as much street credibility. Daddy-O had been knocking cats on their asses for the last couple of years, while E's only claim to fame was being a flunky for any Spanish nigga with a team, and a petty-ass con-man. In the mid to late nineties, E had run with a crew of wild ass Spanish niggaz from 106th that had butted heads with the project crews several times over the last few years. Prince had even taken a bullet during the conflict, so Daddy-O never understood how he could get close with E. Even though E wasn't the kid who shot Prince, he was a part of them. To Daddy-O, E was still the enemy, but he tolerated him on the strength of his friend.

"I didn't know this was a full-service kitchen," Daddy-O said to Prince but kept his eyes on E. "You forget how to cook?" he asked E.

E's eyes glazed over in anger, but he kept his voice neutral. "Not at all, but Prince's whip game is better than mine. I'll be out of your way in a minute so you can have your boss back."

"You got jokes," Daddy-O gave him a dangerous chuckle. "You better keep in mind that I ain't Prince, my dude. Ain't but so much I'm gonna let you slide with."

"Oh, I don't doubt that. And that's why I wouldn't deal with you like I'd deal with Prince. Some cats," E shrugged, "you just can't reason with."

"Yo, why don't you two niggaz both shut up and light something?" Prince interjected, coming over to the table with the dripping cookie clutched between two tongs. He placed the cookie on a glass plate and cut the tiny fan on so it would dry the mix.

"Yeah, that shit is looking right," E said, staring at the cookie. "I can break this shit down and get right at the Hotel."

"You still fucking wit them crackers?" Prince asked.

"Hell yeah, kid. Yo, for what you niggaz get ten for I can get twenty fucking with these cats. One thing I've learned about dealing with these white folks is that they don't mind spending paper on a high, especially if the shit is butter."

"You know you ain't gonna get no bullshit over this side, E," Prince took the chair that sat in the entrance of the kitchen.

"Prince, you ain't gotta say it for me to know it. I know that anything you put in my hand is gonna be proper. That last shit you gave me had the heads bouncing off the walls."

"Yeah, Diego be getting that real deal," Prince said.

"I ain't fucking wit that nigga, son. Ya boy be acting like he's John Gotti or some shit."

"Diego is cool," Prince thought on it. "He's just funny about who he deals with."

"Man, funny is one thing; Diego is paranoid. I tried to pull him to the side the other day to holla at him about some business, and he looked right through me. Then his peoples roll up on me like I'm trying to get at the cat. Ya boy was acting like I was five-O or some shit!"

"Diego is a man that goes with his gut," Daddy-O said sarcastically.

"Don't wet that shit, E, you got what you need right there," Prince pointed to the cookie.

"See, that's why I fuck with you Prince; you're a man that knows how to do business. Yo Diego has got access to all the work in the world, but he ain't gonna be shit because his business sense ain't right. Yo, Prince, I know me and you can go downtown with our own product and get shit popping."

Prince knew that was coming. For the last few months E had been trying to get Prince to make a move with him. He started with the idea of them getting money together in the projects independently, but Prince wasn't really with it. When that didn't work he invited Prince to come down to 59th Street where he was selling crack and coke out of a small hotel off of 12th Avenue. Though the offers sounded very lucrative, Prince always declined.

E probably thought that Prince kept telling him no because he didn't want to dis Diego, but that was only part of the reason. From 100th Street to at least 110th Street Diego was the man, but he ended up being so sort of by default.

Back in the late eighties, early nineties, the streets had turned into a battlefield over crack money. The greed had gotten so out of control that you had dudes making sales on other cat's corners to rope in their customers, totally forgetting the rules of conduct. All of the crews were going at it, trying to become the dominant factors on the west side of Manhattan.

At this time Diego was the second in command to a man named Sonny, who hailed from 201st and Broadway, but got money on 114th and Saint Nicholas. He was a seasoned cat who spoke little English and would let that thing go in a New York minute. He had a small team around him and held his five-block square with authority, until somebody caught him laid up with a broad and put one in his cabbage. His crew eventually disbanded, but Diego continued to make moves here and there, steering clear of the war, and maintaining most of Sonny's old contacts.

In the months that followed, the war started taking heavy casualties. Niggaz was dying, going to jail, or snitching. Either way the numbers on all sides thinned out. Diego had continued to do business with Sonny's connect, so it was easy for him to get his hands on product, but solidifying his position would prove to be a different story. Though most of the original bosses were either killed or doing time, there was still their protégés and predecessors to deal with. A few backdoor deals and the assassination of several key figures, and the competition thinned out considerably. Before you knew it Diego became the man to see if you wanted good coke.

Prince was one of the first to come under Diego's wing when his greedy hand touched Douglass. He started him out pitching but would eventually increase his responsibility. From the beginning Diego saw that Prince was about his money. The fact that he knew damn near the whole projects and brought his own crew to the table made it easier for Diego to move in.

Diego was the kind of dude that would only let a black man rise so far in his organization. Prince was the boss where his crew was concerned, but when it came to Diego's organization as a whole he wasn't that nigga. The executive positions were always reserved for Spanish cats. Diego never said it out loud, but he felt that blacks were mentally inferior. No, both he and E knew that he would never be a boss in that organization, and E often played on that. He thought that if he kept pushing, Prince would come around. He was half right.

Prince knew he would have to bust a move sooner or later, but he wanted it to be on his terms. He wasn't willing to cut off his primary source of income unless he found another one that was more beneficial to him. When he left, it would be on his terms.

"We'll do something together soon, E," Prince said.

E gave him a disbelieving look. "You've been saying that since P.S. 75, poppy. You're out here making a ton of cake for Diego, and he's the only one seeing *real* paper. Son, we're from these projects, so why should we have to settle for scraps off his table?"

"Diego is out here killing 'em, son. Even the cats from 107th ain't clicking like the projects these days," Daddy-O said, reminding them that he was in the room.

Prince gave him a surprised look. He and E tolerated

each other for the sake of him, but there was not a lot of love between them. Having Daddy-O co-sign something E said was unexpected. Maybe it was time to get out from under Diego's thumb, but how? Diego got the coke for the best prices so they couldn't outsell him, and he had more soldiers so they couldn't muscle him out. For as much as he would've loved to be seeing more paper, he refused to sacrifice his team to the soup line.

"I hear you, my nigga," Prince said simply. E and Daddy-O knew to leave it alone, but the idea still hung in the air.

E poked at the cookie with his finger to see if it had dried yet. Satisfied, he dropped it in a baggie and wrapped that in a plastic bag. He took the entire package and stuffed it down his pants. "I'm gonna try to flip this like twice before my son's birthday."

"What's up with little E?" Prince asked.

"That nigga chilling. I was trying to take him to the game the other day, but his mom is on some bullshit. Word, I think that nigga she fuck with be putting shit in her head. Imma fuck him up one day."

"Leave that dude alone, E. I think you just wanna fight him because he's fucking your son's mother," Prince said.

"I don't give a fuck about that bitch," E said defensively. "She could fuck the whole hood and I wouldn't care. I'm just worried about my seed. Yo, little E told me that son be in there play wrestling with him and shit!"

"So what, do you expect him not to like the kid because his father's an asshole?" Prince asked.

"Fuck that," E continued. "That's my seed and ain't gonna be no nigga laying hands on him but me."

Not able to hold his tongue any longer, Daddy-O added his two cents. "Listen to the proud father. Not too long ago you was talking about making her get a paternity test."

Prince shot Daddy-O a look, but he ignored him, keeping his eyes on E's face as it melted into a pool of shit. Daddy-O had touched on a very touchy subject in E's life. Everybody knew what E never seemed to pick up on, that his baby mama was a jump off. For the most part she was faithful to E in their relationship, but she had also had quite a few moments of weakness. E had very pale skin and his son's mother was almost yellow, so when little E came sliding out of the birth canal looking like a chocolate brownie, it raised a few eyebrows. Though E never entertained any of the rumors, he knew they were out there.

"I hear you, son. I guess today must be clown E day?" E said trying to act as if he wasn't infuriated by the statement.

"Come on, E, you know Daddy-O was just fucking wit you, right?" Prince said, trying to defuse the situation. Both the men were his close friends, so he was uncomfortable being tossed into the middle.

E glared at Daddy-O for a few seconds, letting the anger slowly bleed from his eyes. "I don't know, Prince, sometimes Daddy-O doesn't sound like he's joking."

"It's all love, fam," Daddy-O said, less than sincerely. Ignoring E for the moment, Daddy-O put a flame to the end of the blunt and inhaled. The haze was sweet, rolling across his tongue like wisps of cotton candy. The backs of his eyes stung from the smoke, but he held it. Only when it swirled in his chest like storm clouds, threatening to make his heart skip, did he exhale.

"Yo, can I smoke wit y'all niggaz?" Stone called over from the couch. He had to strain a bit to get up from the milk crate. Unlike his brother who was rail thin, Stone was bulky. He was almost as wide as Daddy-O, but not as tall.

"I don't see you burning nothing," Prince nodded to the blunt that was tucked behind Stone's ear.

"You know I pay like I weigh," Stone said, plucking the blunt from behind his ear and placing it between his lips.

"If that was the case your ass would be broke," Daddy-O teased him.

"You don't look like you've missed too many meals," Stone poked him in the gut. "White boy, let me get a light," Stone slapped E on the back way harder than he had to. E just glared at him and handed Stone a book of matches. "Good looking, my nigga."

"Stone, why you play so much?" Prince asked, clearly not feeling the way the younger man had played E.

"Come on, Prince, me and Killa-E play like that all the time."

"Niggaz don't always wanna play, Stone, be easy." Prince's voice was soft, but Stone didn't miss the order beneath the surface. "Oh, did y'all take care of that thing?" Prince distracted everyone from the confrontation to help Stone save face.

Stone's face was suddenly pleasant again. "Yeah, that shit went off real smooth, yo."

"Nigga, stop lying," Sticks called from the door. "Prince, you know Stone had to go overboard with it."

"What done happened now?" Prince asked, taking the blunt that had somehow skipped E.

"Yo, this nigga made son walk home naked!" Sticks went on to recount what he and his brother had subjected the kid to, exaggerating a bit for effect.

"Get the fuck outta here," Daddy-O looked at the twins.

"That's my word, kid, butt ass," Sticks said. "Yo, I wish I could've seen his girl's face when he walked in wit a newspaper wrapped around his ass."

"Yo, y'all some foul niggaz," Prince said. Tears were running down his cheek from laughing so hard.

"Man, that nigga is stupid; there ain't no way in hell I would've walked home naked!" E slapped the table laughing.

"You'd have did whatever the fuck I told you to do if I had that bulldog behind your ear, white boy," Stone told him.

"Fuck outta here," E tried to laugh it off. In the back of his mind he knew that Stone believed what he said. Sticks and Stone were the youngest of the crew, but by far the cruelest. While Sticks was the twisted one, Stone was just brutal. A fine pair they made.

"Prince, I'm 'bout to dip," E said, getting up from the table. "Give me this walk to the elevator," he gave everybody in the room dap, and motioned for his man to follow.

"A'ight," Prince said, coming around through the kitchen. He and E walked down the hall in relative silence. When it was just the two of them E was cool, but when they got around Daddy-O and Stone he tensed up. He knew that E didn't like Daddy-O and was just flat afraid of Stone, but he couldn't really help him with it. You either had to take a stand or be someone's meat, simple as that.

For the most part E was a good nigga. Much like Danny, he wasn't really cut out for the streets, but fate had put him there anyway. E was one of the smartest cats he knew and the dude could've been just about anything in life that he wanted, but he let his dick lead him down the wrong road. E had first started hustling to keep up with his baby mama's taste, but once that rush of power that came from the hustle ran through him, it was a done deal. He had had his little run, but now that it was over he found himself in limbo. The Latinos didn't want him and the blacks didn't trust him.

"Good looking out again on hooking this shit up for me, Prince," E said.

"That ain't nothing, my nigga," Prince patted him on the back. "Mable said that shit is pure fire, so you shouldn't have no problems with it. I'm 'bout to cook a quick fifty more so these niggaz will be good for a minute."

"Prince, let me ask you something. About how much money do you think Diego makes off these projects on a daily basis?"

"Come on, E . . ."

"You know what, don't even answer that," E cut him off. "Just think about the figure, double it, and subtract what you're getting now from it," E stepped on the elevator and smiled at Prince. Before the doors had completely closed he had some parting words. "When you come up with that number you tell me how long it will take *you* to see a million dollars getting one percent of the pie."

■

A few yards south another scene was about to unfold. Gene was a young foot soldier who had only been working for the organization for a few months. He was sixteen with his eyes on the prize and seeing decent money in the projects. He was a quiet kid who never came up short, and Prince could count on him more often than he couldn't to do the right thing.

Gene was sitting on a parked car in the lot, killing time. Business was slow so he figured there wouldn't be any harm in taking a short smoke break. He had scored some boss haze from the Spanish cats down the way and was eager to go to the head on the blunt. Good haze wasn't something you could share with a lot of heads on a blunt and still appreciate. He had taken two good pulls off the blunt when he heard a clicking and felt something cold against his neck.

"That smells like some killa shit," the gunman whispered into Gene's ear. He stepped around so that the young man could see him, but his face was hidden by a mask.

"True indeed," another masked man said, stepping around Gene's left side to stand in front of him. "Set that out," the man ordered, jamming a .38 into Gene's gut. Scared shitless by the thought of being shot, Gene did as he was told.

"What y'all niggaz want?" Gene asked in a shaky voice.

"Don't get cute, son. You know just what we want," the first gunman said, stepping around to where Gene could see him. As he spoke, Gene noticed a faint glint coming from the man's lower teeth. Gene's face remained the same, but he made a mental note of it.

"We need that bread and whatever packs you're holding," the second gunman said.

"Dawg, all I got is some paper and a few loose jacks in my pocket. I ain't get a chance to re-up yet."

Menacing brown eyes stared out from behind the mask of the first gunman as he leaned in to whisper to Gene. "You fucking with me? Yeah, I think you fucking with me," he tapped the barrel of his pistol against Gene's forehead.

"That's word to everything I love, I ain't holding much,"

Gene went to empty his pockets but the second gunman grabbed his wrist.

"Easy," the second gunman warned him. "Wouldn't want you trying to pull out on us." The second gunman emptied Gene's pockets and found about seven loose jacks and a little over a thousand dollars in cash.

"Damn, that's all you holding?" the first gunman asked. Gene nodded, but the gunman didn't believe him. "I think this little nigga is lying." He pointed his gun at Gene's head.

"Son, that's all I got," Gene told him, no longer able to hold back the tears.

The second gunman motioned for the first one to lower his weapon. "Nah, he ain't lying. Gene ain't got the heart to lie at gunpoint."

Gene flinched when the other man called him by name, but neither one of the gunmen seemed to notice. The more he watched their body language the more familiar the gunmen seemed to him. Gene's brain was whirling, but the fear kept him from thinking clearly.

"A'ight, you get to keep your life, but in case you think about trying some funny shit . . ." the first gunman smashed his fist into Gene's face. Gene stumbled but didn't fall. But when the second gunman clobbered him with the butt of the pistol, he crashed to the ground. The last thing Gene remembered before he blacked out was the annoying ass laugh that echoed through the night.

CHAPTER 3

𝕱elix Guzman was a thin Spanish kid with a receding hairline who thought he was God's gift to the game. He was young and getting heavy money off heroin out in Corona, Queens, but two things kept him from reaching that pie in the sky. He couldn't keep his nose out of the product or young pussy. Felix had disregarded the rules of the game he played, thinking that he could make them up as he went along. When you were married to the streets there was only so much she would take before filing for divorce, and unlike most scorned women she didn't want half; she wanted it all. It was a hard lesson that Felix was sure to learn eventually, but for the time being he still managed to keep up the façade of a high-class nigga.

At the present time he was sitting in his brand new Cadillac Escalade smoking a Newport, posted up in front of Monroe Community College, intently watching the young lady who had just exited the school. She had flawless olive skin and long black hair that stopped just above her ass. Her body was something straight out of a workout video, and the whole block noticed her as she passed. Felix smiled at the attention his boo was getting, but quickly threw on his thug face when she hopped in the truck.

"You're late," Felix greeted her.

"Well, hello to you too," she said, brushing a strand of hair from her eye.

"You got that for me?" he asked, reaching for her knapsack.

"Hold the fuck on," she snatched the bag out of his reach. "You gonna pull it out right here in front of the school? Pull around the corner."

Felix was tempted to bust her in her mouth to let her know just who was boss in the relationship, but he played nice because he needed something from her. Once he got what he wanted, he was going to remind her who was running the show. Felix just smiled and did as he was told. They made two rights and pulled into a parking spot on a residential block. Felix put the car in park and looked over at his passenger.

"Here," she said, tossing him a paper bag. "I don't see why you couldn't just come by the apartment to get it instead of having me carry it around all day in school."

"Cause I got some moves to make in the Bronx, and I

didn't feel like coming all the way to Queens just to have to ride back here."

"I could've got knocked with that shit."

"But you didn't," he said, peeking into the bag. His leg shook involuntarily as he eyed the ounce of uncut heroin.

"So, are you gonna take me home? I hopped on the train instead of driving my car cause I didn't want to get pulled over holding that shit," She told him.

Felix looked at her as if he hadn't heard the question. "What? Take you home? Nah, I can't do that, ma. I told you that I got moves to make. Hop back on the train; the ride ain't that long."

"Felix, you know I gotta take two trains and a bus to get home. That shit is gonna take me like two hours!" she shouted.

"Who the fuck is you talking to?" he leaned over so that they were nose to nose. "I'll break ya fucking neck." He drew his hand back and she curled up in the corner, fearing the blow that never fell. "You're fucking spoiled, that's your problem. That fucking brother of yours has you thinking that your shit doesn't stink."

"Don't talk about my brother!" she said heatedly.

"And what the fuck are you gonna do, tell on me? While you're at it why don't you tell him what we've been doing behind his back." She remained silent. "That's what the fuck I thought. You need to relax, shorty."

She folded her arms and glared at Felix. Tears wanted to stream down her face, but she had decided that she had shed enough tears for Felix's ass. "What, I'm not supposed to be uptight? Felix, you were supposed to be flipping what I gave you, but you haven't brought back straight money yet. We gotta get this right before . . ."

Felix slapped her before she could finish her sentence. "Who the fuck do you think you're talking to? I know just what the fuck I took and what I'm supposed to bring back. What, you think cause you helped a nigga get his ones up that I owe you something? You better remember who you're talking to."

"You didn't have to hit me," she sobbed.

"Well, stay your ass up outta my mix. Listen," he softened his tone, "I'm sorry I hit you, but you just made me a little angry," he stroked her cheek. "You let me worry about getting the money right, and you just go back to the crib and get pretty for me. Daddy is gonna come knock the bottom out that pussy tonight, smell me?"

"Whatever," she said, hopping out of the truck and slamming the door.

"Bitch!" Felix flexed like he was about to jump out, but the girl had already made hurried steps to the curb. "See, that's the kind of shit that makes me go upside your head, you spoiled little cunt!" Felix threw the truck in gear and peeled off.

The girl just shook her head. For the thousandth time she

wondered what the hell she was doing with Felix's tired ass. Her brother had warned her against getting involved with one of his business associates, but she was hardheaded. Felix had stolen her heart, and she allowed that to lead her instead of good common sense. She had tried to convince herself that Felix really loved her and that the drugs made him lash out, but she knew it was a lie. All he cared about was what she could do for him.

Her China doll eyes threatened to storm, and it was only her strength of will that held the waterworks at bay. Felix wasn't worth the tears. If he wanted to show his ass, that was fine with her, but that didn't mean she had to stand for it. As far as she was concerned the shop was closed, and Felix could settle his own debts. She had covered for him long enough. Felix thought he was slicker than a pig in shit, but little did either one of them know he was living on borrowed time.

■

"He's pulling off, you wanna get at him now?" the driver asked his passenger.

The man sitting in the passenger seat took slow drags from his cigarette. He thought about just snatching Felix and getting it over with, but decided to wait. He wanted to drop the curtain on the turncoat and his thieving-ass girlfriend at the same time.

"Nah," the passenger exhaled the cigarette smoke. "We'll get the mutha fucka though. Pull off."

■

Prince and Daddy-O weren't feeling much pain when they came out of the building. During the time it took them to cook the fifty grams of cocaine they had probably smoked about five bombers of sweet haze. They had left Sticks and Stone to chop and bag the rock while they went to see what mischief they could get into.

The block was popping that night. The grills were still going and the number of people that had been in the court-yard had doubled. There were so many people out that night that the police couldn't tell who was slinging and who was just hanging, so they fell back, at least for the moment. Someone had run an extension cord from their house and there were two stereos going at full volume. The projects were in full swing.

"Yo, I'm hungry as hell," Daddy-O rubbed his gut.

"Nigga, you always hungry." Prince threw two phantom punches at Daddy-O. "Nah, but I got the munchies too."

"Yo, lets hit the chicken spot and head uptown to see what up wit them hoes," Daddy-O suggested.

"I don't know, kid, this product ain't gonna move itself," Prince said.

"Nigga, get off that shit. You got at least five niggaz on

deck right now; the product will be alright without you. Let's hit the strip club and see about getting some pussy or something."

"Man, we supposed to be stacking paper, not blowing it," Prince told him.

Daddy-O shook his head. "Look, tomorrow is the first. Whatever we blow tonight we'll make it up on the come around." Seeing the hesitant look on Prince's face, Daddy-O pressed it. "My dude, how long has it been since we went out and got stupid? Let's take this shit back to 2002," Daddy-O nudged him. "But yo, lets go over there and see what Keisha got popping on the grill." Daddy-O nodded toward the benches.

Keisha was a short chick with cocoa skin and wore her hair in a bob-cut. She was one of the few chicks that hung around the crew but no one tried to fuck. She was like one of the fellas as far as Prince and Daddy-O were concerned. There was a rumor that she had given Stone some pussy back in the days, but neither of them had ever admitted to it.

"Keish, Keish," Daddy-O sang, smiling at the girl who was turning a pork link on the grill.

"What's good, Daddy-O?" she nodded.

"One of them burgers," he said.

"Damn, nigga do you do anything besides beg?"

"Sure, I knock the bottom outta pussies." He busted up laughing. "But what's up with one of them burgers though, for real, ma?"

"Here, wit yo fat ass," she slapped a burger on a bun and handed it to him. "You want one, Prince?"

"Only if you got it to spare," he said.

"She got it, my nigga," Daddy-O said, stuffing the last of his burger into his mouth.

"Shut up, Daddy-O. I know one thing, you better have some money for a bitch the way your fat ass is slamming those burgers."

"Prince of the ghetto!" a familiar voice called from behind them. The three of them turned around at the same time to see Scatter shambling towards them. Scatter was a dude who had lived in the projects longer than either Prince or Daddy-O had been alive. He was around their mothers' ages but always kept the lines of communication open with the young boys. His yellow face, which at times seemed to be dripping off his skull, was pocked and bore the signs of a hard life. His trademark shopping bag hung from his thin arm, weighed down with God only knew what. Scatter was one of the hood's most seasoned boosters. Dressed in a three-piece olive colored suit and matching snakeskin shoes, you wouldn't know he was an addict unless someone told you.

"What it do, y'all?" Scatter asked, giving both the men pounds.

"Ain't nothing, Scat," Prince said. "What you getting into?"

"Out here shucking and jiving, trying to get this monkey off my back, dig?" he replied, scratching his neck.

"You know we got that good-good in the building, son; go see my little man." Daddy-O told him.

"Yeah, yeah, I know. I'm just trying to get my money up so I can go cop me a taste. Then I'm going uptown to get me a bag of that poison. You know I gotta get my cocktail on."

"Boy you love running in the fast lane with that dope-coke combo. What, that white don't get you right?" Daddy-O asked.

"Shiiit, barely. Man, y'all know I ain't no mutha fucking coke head by nature. I like to dance with the devil."

"Yeah, dope was the shit back in y'all day, kid."

"It was more than the shit; it was God to some of us. Man, a good hit of dope is sweeter than head from the most skilled bitch!" Scatter said, doing a little dance.

"Well if the shit is so good, why even bother with the coke?" Prince asked.

"Ah," Scatter twirled, "that's the sixty-four-thousand-dollar question. Back in the days if you had some boss dope, you had the world at your fingers. This paper y'all see off crack ain't shit to a dope man's bag."

"So what the fuck happened to the dope game, in all its glory?" Daddy-O asked, sarcastically.

"Same thing that happened to the real coke game; we let the young boys play it, and they ruined it. There used to be rules to this shit, but the greedy mutha fuckas running the show now ain't got no sense of honor. Back in my day every mutha fucka holding a good bag was nigger rich, but that was a long time ago." He schooled them.

"Yo, I remember hearing stories about niggaz becoming millionaires off that shit," Prince said.

"What you hear is the real deal, my man. Dope money is sweet as honey. Shiiit, ask Diego; he'll tell you. The only reason that snake ain't flooded the hood wit that shit is probably because he ain't got a good connect, cause he was damn sure out here when it was jumping. When dope was the thing, the street was paved with gold, Jack," Scatter said with a dreamy look in his eyes. He drifted for a second before he remembered why he had even run up on the two of them. "Check it though, I know you niggaz is trying to get drunk this weekend, so pony up the bread and let me hook you up?"

"What you got, Scat?" Daddy-O asked, looking at the bag.

Scatter rummaged around in the shopping bag and came up holding a bottle of champagne and a magnum of Hennessy. "I'll let the yak go for fifty, but I need at least a sixty-cent for the bubbles. You know that Roseau ain't cheap."

"Come on, Scat, let ya boy rock for the thirty-five," Daddy-O protested, clutching the magnum by the neck of the bottle.

"Daddy-O, why we gotta go through this shit every time we do business? I give y'all niggaz better deals than I do anybody else, but you still try to Jew me. Come on, man."

"A'ight, I'll give you forty-cent for it," Daddy-O said,

fishing two twenties out of his pocket and dangling it in front of Scatter.

"Fuck it, you cheap bastard." Scatter snatched the two twenties from Daddy-O's hand. "But the least you could do is throw me a bag for fucking me up the ass."

"You got that, my nigga," Daddy-O said, placing the bottle on the bench.

"What about you, Prince; you gonna cop that bottle?" Scatter asked, now anxious to spend the forty dollars he had just earned and collect on his free bag.

Prince was staring at the bottle, but his mind was elsewhere. "Huh?"

"The bottle, man, what's good?"

"Oh, a'ight, let me get that." Prince handed him three twenties.

"My nigga, can't get no bigger," Scatter sang, slapping his palm. "Yo, I got some fly-ass silk shirts coming in this week too, see about me my nigga!" Scatter said, gliding toward the building.

"Whatever, nigga," Prince said. He watched Scatter slink away with his words of wisdom still ringing in the back of his mind.

"Well, since y'all niggaz is going in on my grill, let a bitch go in on the bottle," Keisha said, grabbing three cups from the shopping cart that was leaning against the gate.

Daddy-O filled his, Keisha's, and Prince's cup to the line with the dark liquor. Prince and Daddy-O took deep swigs but were upstaged when Keisha downed her cup in one shot. She made a fuck-face and tossed the cup into the trash. It was said that Keisha could outdrink most niggaz in the hood, and watching her throw the cup back was proof of that.

"You better be careful with that," Prince teased her.

"Nigga, this ain't gonna do nothing but take the edge off. Me and my bitches is stepping out tonight, and I need to be drunk when we get there. You know the drinks in the club be too damn high," Keisha informed them.

"Word, what's going on tonight?" Daddy-O asked.

"It my girl Sharon's twenty-first birthday, so we're going to the Sugar Shack."

"Sharon with the phat ass?"

Keisha looked at Daddy-O and shook her head. "Nigga, you is too thirsty. Yeah, that Sharon."

"Yeah, we need to see about that, kid," Daddy-O rubbed his meaty hands together. "What time y'all rolling?"

Keisha checked the time on her cell phone. "Probably another hour or two."

"Cool, that'll give us some time to make our rounds and change clothes. What's good, my dude," he turned to Prince. "We at the Sugar Shack?"

Prince looked around at the bustling projects and weighed the sight against the last time he had stepped out with his man. "Fuck it," he shrugged.

CHAPTER 4

Prince and Daddy-O exited the projects on 103rd and headed north on Columbus Avenue. The avenue was just as alive with people as the interior of the projects. Kids mobbed around the ice-cream truck spending their parents' money on belly aches and bad teeth, happy to be free of their hot-ass houses after dark. Several young men were huddled on the side steps of the center shooting dice. They all acknowledged Prince and Daddy-O as they walked by. The two were legends in the projects, and all the young dudes wanted to grow up to be like them.

"What you think about that dope shit ya man was kicking?" Prince asked Daddy-O.

"Man, you know Scatter be talking out his ass. That shit was like the seventies or eighties when that shit was popping. Once that freebase came around, it was a wrap."

"I don't know, man, you see how old Blue on it, and I

know fo sho he was moving that D back in his day," Prince said.

"Yeah, that mutha fucka is still sitting on paper, but Blue been in and out the game since the sixties," Daddy-O reminded him.

"Maybe I should holla at Diego about it?"

"Prince, you can do what you want, but you know he ain't gonna wanna hear about setting up no dope spots in the projects. He's too stuck on the fast paper that comes from crack and coke. It's a quick turnaround with minimal hassle for his lazy ass."

"True," Prince said. Daddy-O was right. Diego was a nigga who was set in his ways and didn't like to deviate. Dope was a gamble worth taking, but Diego wasn't gonna go for it, and Prince didn't have the paper or connect to try it on his own. Their conversation was broken up when E came across the street.

"What's good, son? Where y'all headed?" E asked.

" 'Bout to see who's up the block," Prince told him.

"Yo, you think that little nigga with the nicks of haze is out there? I'm trying to get right."

"He should be," Prince shrugged. "Come on." The duo had now become a threesome as they headed up the block.

When they crossed 104th street, the age range went up a bit. Project veterans from several different eras could be found on this corner hanging around like their names still held weight. Daddy-O and Prince called the corner *The Hustler's Boneyard*. Most of the cats who hung on this corner were washed up in the game, but still held on to the fleeting memories that had once defined their lives.

"Young Prince, what it do?" a retired hustler named Oscar called out. He was wearing a pair of leather shorts and a black tank top. Back in the day Oscar had made a pretty penny on the streets, but several bullets and multiple prison terms had forced him into retirement.

"I can't call it, man." Prince shrugged his shoulders. "I'm trying to be like you when I grow up."

"Never like me, baby, always better. You remember who told you that. Daddy-O," Oscar turned his attention to Prince's partner and fake jabbed at him. "You still out here sitting niggaz on their asses?"

"Hey, man, I do what I do," Daddy-O said modestly. Though he was much younger than Oscar and the others, most of them respected him as one of their peers. Daddy-O was nice with his hands and had been knocking grown men out since he was a shorty. Had life been kinder, he could've had a successful career as a boxer, but the streets had claimed his heart along with his dreams.

"Spoken like a true G," Oscar said, sipping something dark from a plastic cup. "Man, y'all niggaz remind me of me and my crew back in the days. Me, Black, and Greg used to have all the bitches and all the money."

"Yeah, y'all made a few dollars out here, but me and my nigga got you beat on the hoes. We knocking 'em out the box left and right."

"Boy, you must've fell and bumped your head. I had more hoes than Wilt and twice as much game!" Oscar declared in a booming voice.

"Que pasa, fellas, what's all the yelling about?" a short Hispanic cat said, coming out of the bodega. He was dressed in a pair of black linen pants and a loud orange button up. The offensive color pattern looked as if someone had broken open a magic marker and flicked it at him. His hair had begun to thin in the front, but he still rocked it in a close fade, struggling to hold on to the memories of having a full head of hair. With a pencil mustache and dreamy eyes, the man wasn't a very intimidating sight, but when you had that kind of power you didn't have to be. Diego controlled the cocaine trade around the neighborhood, therefore the wolves were at his call. One of the most vicious wolves trailed him like a shadow.

Manny was a man of few words and few enemies. Probably because he had killed most of them off. Like E, he had been a part of the old regime, but unlike E, Manny knew how to make himself useful to the new one. If you ever wanted someone dealt with in true straight-to-DVD fashion, you called Manny. He'd blow your head off at your mother's house, flee to PR, then sneak back into the country when the heat died down. Even with the heightened homeland security, there were still ways for niggaz that had been doing it long enough.

Prince gave Diego a pound/hug. "Wasn't 'bout nothing; we just out here clowning with Oscar."

"Seems like you niggaz do more clowning than grinding. Take a walk with me to the liquor store, Prince." Diego steered Prince north on Columbus Avenue, speaking softly into his ear. Manny brought up the rear, toking on a Newport, with Daddy-O at his side and E a few paces back. They had gone about a half block before Diego looked over his shoulder and stopped short.

"Fuck is you going?" he asked E.

"Huh?" he asked, confused.

"I don't recall asking you to come along."

"Come on, D." Prince tried to speak on E's behalf, but Diego wasn't trying to hear it.

"Nah, fuck that, Prince. I know that's ya man, but I don't like this sneaky little mutha fucka," Diego said honestly.

"Diego, why you acting like that, fam?" E asked, as if he didn't know he wasn't one of Diego's least favorite people.

"E, don't play stupid with me. You might have Prince fooled with this underdog shit, but I know you. I was there when you was fucking with niggaz from up the block, and I know how you move. Nah, poppy, be on ya way."

"Yo, you be on some bullshit!" E said a little more heatedly than he meant to. As soon as he saw Manny move he regretted his words.

"You feeling brave?" Manny hissed. He was so close up on E that spittle rained on the shorter man's face.

"Yo, go ahead with that, Manny," E said, raising his hand to try and keep some distance between himself and Diego's pet sociopath. He never saw Manny move, but he knew he was in trouble when pain shot up through his arm. Manny had grabbed E about the wrist and twisted until the bones threatened to snap.

"Fuck is you stupid or something?" Manny asked, slapping E viciously in the back of the head. "Don't even raise your fucking hands to me!" This time he swung from underneath the stooped man and slapped him in the mouth. Blood flew from E's lips and dotted the concrete.

"Chill, Manny!" Prince moved to break it up, but Diego held him back.

"Cool out, poppy. I know that's ya man, but don't draw lines in the sand," Diego said seriously.

Prince looked into Diego's eyes and saw the threat beneath the words. There was no doubt in his mind that if he put himself out there for E, his business with Diego would be done, not to mention that he stood a good chance of winding up on his shit list. Prince wasn't afraid of Diego, but he held no illusions in his mind about what the man was capable of. He might take out a few foot soldiers, but that would be about as far as it went before Diego's soldiers crushed Prince's crew. E was cool, but not worth risking his entire team over. Angrily, Prince stayed where he was and watched Manny slap E up.

The beating only lasted a few seconds, but it seemed like an eternity for E who was on the receiving end. Manny hadn't yet hit him with a closed fist, but he slapped the shit out of E every time his face opened up. E's face was so on fire that even after Diego had called Manny off, he still felt like he was being slapped.

"E, you a'ight?" Prince asked, trying to help him keep his feet under him.

"I'm good." E jerked away from Prince. He spat a wad of blood from his mouth and just stared at it as if he wasn't sure if it was his or not. He hadn't meant to be so harsh with Prince, but he was uptight at Diego and Prince by association. He knew Prince's hands were tied in the matter. E was just getting a good slapping around, but if Prince tried to step in, Diego would look at it as betrayal and surely send the death squad for his protégé.

"Stand that nigga up so I can tag his ass again," Manny taunted as he danced around throwing phantom punches.

"That's enough!" Prince shouted.

"What? Nigga, fuck you, who you think you're talking to? I'll kick your black ass too!"

Anger danced through Prince. It was bad enough he had to sit and watch E catch a bad one, but he would be damned if Manny would come at him sideways. Diego's boy or not, Prince was gonna whip his ass.

"Okay, okay," Diego stepped between them. "No need for two of my best guys to be going at it. Manny," he turned to his bodyguard. "You've proved your point, so chill. If you and Prince wanna tear each other up, you'll do it in the ring, not on the street like two common fucking punks." No matter how heated they were, both men knew better than to argue with Diego. They'd let it go for now, but a reckoning was sure to come of the incident.

"E, let me walk you to your building," Prince offered, momentarily forgetting about Manny, who was still glaring at him.

"I'm good, P, word," E told him. He cast angry eyes over to Diego, who was watching Prince. If E had a pistol on him, he'd have gunned Diego and Manny down, but he had foolishly come out unarmed. It was a mistake he wouldn't make again.

"Dawg, you sure?" Prince asked.

E let his eyes linger on Diego and Manny for a second or two longer before answering Prince. "Yeah, man. I know how it is," he nodded at Diego. "Go handle ya business. Me and homeboy will settle up sooner or later." E licked his wounds and slunk back to the other side of the projects.

CHAPTER 5

Sticks sat on the bench where Keisha had previously been grilling, watching any and everyone. Not long ago word had come down about Gene getting robbed by two unknown men, and he wasn't happy about it. Gene was a good kid whom Sticks had taken a liking to, so he took it quite personal when the robber broke Gene's jaw. His little man was laid up in the hospital getting his shit wired, and somebody would have hell to pay because of it.

"What the hell is wrong with you?" Danny asked, noticing the murderous look in Sticks's eyes.

"Ain't nothing, just trying to stay on point," Sticks said dryly. Danny was a part of their team, but he wasn't one of Sticks's favorite people.

"Man, y'all tripping. Them niggaz ain't gonna come back around here knowing that we're onto them."

"And how the fuck do you know? You got the inside track?" Sticks asked coldly. His unnaturally black eyes sent a chill down Danny's spine.

"Hell nah, I'm just saying. These niggaz out here know that we 'bout that homicide. They ain't gonna try it again," Danny boasted.

"Dig this." Sticks sat up. "Whoever moved on Gene knew exactly when and where to get him, so that means they've been watching him, which also means that they know who he's with and don't give a fuck."

"Man, I better not find out who it is, cause if I do I'm gonna dumb the fuck out!" Danny declared. Sticks just looked at him and went back to surveying the projects.

A few minutes later Shakes walked up. She was decked out in a one piece spandex suit and a pair of crunchy Reebok classics. "Yo, Sticks, let me get with you for a minute."

Sticks looked around before getting up and walking over to Shakes. She whispered something in his ear to which he just nodded. Sticks handed her a small nugget of crack wrapped in foil and headed back to the bench.

"Let ya boy know something," Danny said, knowing that Shakes probably had a lead on whoever the robbers were.

"Just be cool; I got this under control," Sticks said, pulling out his cell phone to call his brother.

■

"That shit wasn't called for," Prince said to Diego after E had gone.

"Says you. That nigga know I don't fuck with him so why would he even try to tag along. Fuck him, Prince. That kid is rotten, and you need to stop fucking with him."

"That's my peoples," Prince defended.

Diego looked at him sadly. "If that's ya peoples then ya got a real short career ahead of you." Prince gave Diego a confused look, so Diego decided to explain, which was something he rarely did. "Prince, that nigga E is rotten, no good to the game. He's a bottom-feeder, the kind of mutha fucka that will ride with you for as long as you're useful, but when the shit hits the fan he's gonna vanish. See, he talks that street shit and even tries to act the part, with them simple-ass Spanish niggaz he keeps around, but you and I know he ain't built like that."

"Nah, man. E is straight. He was getting money with niggaz on 106th for the longest." Prince continued to defend E.

"Yeah, and when they all got knocked where the fuck was E? That was probably the only nigga that skated off without a scratch."

Prince thought about it for a minute. Damn near fifty people in total went down when the police rushed the Dominicans, but E managed to be out of town on the day it happened. There were speculations about E's convenient absence during the bust, but Prince had known him for years and couldn't see it.

"Nah, I think you got him wrong."

"And you're a good judge of character all of a sudden?" Diego raised his eyebrow. "Look I ain't even about to start on you and your fucking trigger-happy-ass stooges."

"Call us what you want, but we command respect in our fucking hood," Prince said seriously.

"You hear this nigga, Manny?" he asked his shadow and was answered with a chuckle. "Let me ask you something," he turned back to Prince, "what the fuck have y'all niggaz done over here to *command* anything?" Prince made to answer, but Diego cut him off. "Son, you out here making a lot of paper for a nigga your age, but you and your crew are still green to a lot of shit. Think about how reckless those little mutha fuckas are. The guns, the fights, the traffic, all that shit makes you hot. If you ever wanna be somebody in this game, you gotta run a tight house, poppy."

Prince's first instinct was to remind Diego who had set *his* house in order as far as the projects went, but he didn't. He was tight, but he wouldn't give Diego the satisfaction of showing it. With niggaz who had big egos, you had to cater to them. But ego or not Prince saw their open conversation as an opportunity to put his bid in.

"D, I hear what you're saying and you know I value your advice, but I got this," Prince said. He saw Diego's eye twitch and continued hurriedly. "With all due respect, I'm out here with these niggaz everyday, so I know their strengths and weaknesses. I know who I can give rope to and who I can't.

D, have I ever come to you with short money or letting my team's bullshit spill over onto yo shit?"

"Prince, I see you going somewhere with this. What's good, poppy?" Diego asked, finally.

"I want in," Prince said flatly. Diego opened his mouth, but Prince held his hand up. "My dude, I've been out here getting it up for the team for a long time, but sometimes it feels like I'm running in place. Man, shit is sweet, but it could be sweeter if you let a nigga ball."

Diego looked at him with a crooked grin. "Prince, if I didn't know any better, I'd think you weren't happy with my family. Is that what you're telling me?"

"Hell nah, man. You know I fucks wit you, hard body." Prince assured him. "I'm just asking for a little creative freedom. Look, we can do it like you did with the boy, Dante."

Dante, like Prince, was once one of Diego's crew bosses that eventually earned his freedom, so to speak. Diego allowed Dante to operate independently on Amsterdam Avenue. He would be the boss of his turf and those under him, but he could only buy coke from Diego at about three dollars higher per gram than everyone else. To top it off Diego also enforced a street tax that had to be paid once a month. Diego called it *paying homage*, but robbery was robbery no matter how you said it. The upside was that even with the street tax, you still had the freedom to get your weight up.

Diego shrugged his shoulders. "Dante was a special case. Prince, why you wanna break from the family? You're twenty-two years old and running damn near the whole projects. You got money and respect. Don't I take care of you?"

"That's the point, D; *I* wanna take care of me. Son, what we got is love so it ain't gotta change; I just wanna have a little more freedom to make some change. A nigga don't wanna live in the projects forever."

"Okay, okay," Diego clapped his hands together. "You want more power; I'll give it to you. I'm trying to muscle these niggaz from 93rd and Amsterdam out on some weed shit. When I knock these niggaz out the box, I'll let you take over the crack houses. That'll be your little piece of the rock, just make sure my money don't get funny."

Prince looked at Diego. "D, that'd be cool for someone just coming in, but at the end of the day, it's still *your* shit. I'm knee deep in this, so I need room to move around. I was thinking that maybe we could work something out for the Columbus side of the projects?"

"Columbus?" Diego asked in disbelief. "Prince, you know I can't do that."

"Come on, D, I grew up on that side. Who better to hold it down than me?" Prince reasoned.

"I feel you, Prince, and had you asked for any other block we could've worked something out. I make too much money on that side to give it up. Nah," Diego shook his head. "You can eat off my plate for as long as you like, but you ain't getting your own fork. That's *my* hood." Diego said, finally.

From the corner of his eyes, Prince could see Daddy-O

looking to him for a sign. Manny must've felt the tension too, because he moved closer to the two men. Staring into Diego's eyes made Prince feel like an invisible force was trying to drive him to his knees, but he was his own man and wouldn't bend. Still it didn't make sense to put himself on Diego's shit list. After all, he was still the boss.

"Don't feel no way about it though, Prince," Diego's face softened. "Back when I was your age I couldn't wait to grow up, until I got old and wanted my youth back. Come on, man." Diego threw his arm around Prince's shoulders and tried steering him into the liquor store. "Let's go in here and get some champagne. Tomorrow we'll talk about getting you set up on 94th."

"I think I'll pass on the drink, my nigga." Prince gave him a hug and a pound/hug.

"Prince, I know you ain't acting like that over some coke blocks?" Diego spread his arms.

"Nah, D, you know I understand this business," Prince shrugged. "Me and my man is gonna get up outta here and chase a little trim."

Diego gave him a broad smile. "Hmm, a hunt for the cunt, those were the fucking days." Diego thought back a few years. "Yo, Manny," he turned to the slightly taller man who was silently watching everyone. "Remember how sweet the pussy chasing was when we were these guys' age?"

"Not really, I was locked up from the time I was eighteen until I turned twenty-five," Manny said seriously.

"Whatever," said Prince, disregarding his comment. "Yo," he turned back to Prince and Daddy-O. "Y'all niggaz be careful out there; the streets is dangerous in the summer."

"Please believe it," Prince said seriously, before disappearing down the block with Daddy-O on his heels.

■

"Guess you ain't gonna holla at him about that heroin," Daddy-O said, glaring at the backs of Diego and Manny as they left the liquor store and headed back in the direction of the projects.

Prince lit a cigarette and spat on the ground. "Guess not."

CHAPTER 6

Once you crossed 104th street, the projects ended, giving way to bodegas, beauty salons, and tenement buildings. Granted, the tenements on Columbus Avenue weren't as run down as some of the ones further up in Harlem, but they still weren't much to look at. Inside of an apartment on the top floor of one of these tenements, Diego sat with his ever present shadow, Manny.

The apartment they sat in was one that only a few of Diego's closest soldiers had access to. Though Diego sometimes slept there, it wasn't his home, just one of several places he had to get low. A deep burgundy carpet stretched from one end of the living room to the other, stopping just before the foyer. The furniture was very basic. A sofa and love seat with a forty-two-inch television. On the surface it was a very normal looking apartment, but in the game, nothing was ever as it appeared to be. Behind an iron door, to which only Diego had a key, was a veritable arsenal of weapons of all shapes and sizes. The apartment was what they called their *armory*.

"You should've let me eat that nigga, D," Manny said from across the kitchen table. He was busy chopping the lumps out of a pile of cocaine with a twenty-five-cent razor. In his free hand he held a straw that had been cut down to a quarter of its original size. Pinching one nostril, Manny dipped the straw into the powder and inhaled.

"Who, E?" Diego asked, pouring whiskey into a plastic cup. He downed the liquor and chased it with the Corona he had been drinking.

"Nah, Prince. Yo, he frogged up like he wanted to do something."

"That wasn't about shit, Manny. He was just trying to protect his man."

"Fuck that. I wouldn't care if that was his brother. You told that nigga to fall back, and he should've stayed the fuck out of it." Manny slid the plate over to Diego.

"I'm not stunting it, so why are you?" Diego asked before taking his turn with the *white lady*.

"Because that monkey needs to know his place." Manny slammed his fist against the table, nearly spilling the coke and the liquor. A sharp look from Diego told him to calm his ass down. "Listen, poppy, that nigga Prince is getting too big for his fucking britches."

"Why, because he actually stood up to you? That took big balls."

"Big balls and a tiny brain. I should've stomped the shit out of him!" Manny said.

Diego gave him a mocking grin. "I don't know, Manny. I've seen Prince get down, and the boy knows how to throw them thangs."

"You actually think that Prince can whip my ass, D?" Manny asked, clearly offended. "A'ight, wait till next time I see him, and then we'll see."

"Chill, I'm just fucking wit you. Nah, but don't take that shit personal, dawg. Prince is young, and youth sometimes makes us do dumb shit, feel me?"

"You got a point there. There's no way I would've put my ass in the fire for that snitching-ass faggot E."

"Me neither, but what am I gonna do about it? I told Prince and it's up to him to take the advice. I just hope he wises up before that snake bites him on the ass and fucks up my flow."

"If he ends up dragging Prince into some shit, we'll just get someone to replace him. Prince ain't the fucking MVP of this team."

Diego just gave his friend a look.

"D, I know you ain't thinking about bumping this nigga up?" Manny asked in disbelief. "You'd actually consider letting that baboon sit at this table?" Manny wasn't very fond of black people, black men especially.

It all stemmed back to his days as a kid, when he was little Manny, the Puerto Rican immigrant, instead of a feared killer. Manny and his family came from PR with nothing but the clothes on their back. Their first home was in the Bronx's Jackson projects, which was predominantly black at the time. The black kids always made fun of his clothes and called him names, making his childhood a living hell. As a preteen, Manny tried to sell drugs but ended up getting locked up within the first month. During his six-month stay in the juvenile detention center, Manny was subjected to ungodly horrors, including being gang raped by a group of black kids. No one knew his secret, including his best friend Diego, but it would shape the man he was to become. From that moment on, he decided that he would make all blacks pay for what the group of boys did to him.

"Manny, you need to chill. I ain't got a lot of love for the cocolos either, but we're all niggaz at the end of the day. Let's just get this fucking money, kid!" Diego told him.

"I hear you talking, D, but I don't know if I like the idea of you letting Prince in. We can't have shit without the blacks wanting a piece of the action. That's why all them niggaz had to get laid down so we could do us."

Something else few people knew were the details of how Diego solidified his hold on the Westside. During the aftermath of the turf wars, Diego and Manny had orchestrated and carried out a series of hits, eliminating anyone who could've been considered rivals to his claim. Lieutenants, second in commands, even some of the eldest sons of the old bosses were whacked. It didn't matter if you were active in the game or not, if you had a stake you had to die. That's just how it went. Had anyone put two and two together, Diego's life would've been forfeit for the innocent teenagers he murdered, but he was never even a suspect. When the smoke cleared, he was the boss of the Westside.

"Watch your fucking mouth!" Diego looked around nervously. "Why don't you tell the whole fucking world we whacked out those guys?" The third of their trio was in the other room, but you could never be too cautious when it came to ear-hustling.

Realizing his mistake, Manny lowered his voice. "Look, all I'm saying is that I don't think it's a good idea for you to give Prince more power than he already has. Those hood-rat mutha fuckas follow him like the Pied Piper as it is."

"I don't pay you to think; I pay you to kill," Diego said seriously. "Listen, I watched that kid go from a snot-nosed punk to one of my best earners. Prince is the reason why our hold over the projects is so strong. He's more valuable to the team than he gives himself credit for, but I'd never tell him that. The boy is getting his weight up so I'd think there was something wrong if he didn't want to move up. I'm not saying I plan on giving him as much power as my other lieutenants have, but it wouldn't hurt to give him a taste of what it's like. Kinda like stroking his ego, ya know? Once we clean out that spot on nine-four, I'm gonna let him and his ragamuffins have it."

"If you say so, D," Manny reluctantly agreed.

"I do."

"I hope y'all saved some of that for me," Benny said coming out of the bedroom. Benny plopped in one of the empty kitchen chairs and snatched up the other half of Manny's straw. He was short and plump with smooth brown skin. Benny and Diego had come up together under Sonny, but it was Benny's craving for coke and women that had stunted his growth in the game. Benny had been a loyal lieutenant to Sonny, as he was with Diego, but lacked the leadership qualities that you would expect to find in someone who had over fifteen years on the streets. The coke made him crazy and sometimes unreasonable, thus no one was willing to follow him. The only reason that he had managed to live through the turf wars while most of Sonny's other lieutenants died off was because he was locked up at the time. Any chance that Benny had had at the brass ring was a memory, so he found himself in the position of Diego's yes-man and head chef.

"Jesus, Benny, you're gonna burn your sinuses out!" Manny warned, watching Benny snort two thick lines of coke, lumps and all.

"I got this, amigo," Benny snorted to clear his sinuses.

"I've been doing this shit since you were in pampers, right, D?"

"Yeah, this nigga has been bumping since we were kids," Diego admitted. "Manny's got a point though, Benny. This new shit ain't like the powder we came up on. Even though this ain't been stepped on," he motioned toward the coke on the table, "it's still got a lot of extra shit in it."

"Fuck it, my nigga. We can't live forever anyway." Benny sniffed two more thick lines. His nose began to drip onto the table, splattering the pile in front of him. "You want some more of this, bro?" Benny asked Manny in a nasally tone. There was powder caked in and around his nose, making him sound like he had a cold.

"I'm good for now," Manny raised his hands. There was something about getting high with Benny that made him feel like an addict.

"Yo, while you busy in here snorting my shit up, did you finish whipping that for me?" Diego asked, getting back to business.

"I got you, poppy. I'll be finished by sometime tonight."

"Tonight? Benny, I gave you that coke yesterday, fuck are you over here doing?"

"D, you know how long it takes to cook a half a bird, man. Even as nice as I am, it still takes a while, poppy. You know I got you though."

"Benny, sometimes I don't even know why I fuck with you," Diego got up from the table and stretched.

"Because there ain't been a nigga as nice as me on the cook-up since Sonny, God bless." Benny made the sign of the cross. He raised a very good point. There were several people in Diego's organization that knew the formula to turn cocaine to crack-rock, but only a select few could be called nice. Benny could literally turn shit to sugar and get an extra few grams out of it in the process. No one really knew how he did it, because Benny never let anyone watch him cook, including Diego. That made sure that he remained valuable to Diego and would always have a job.

"Just make sure you get it done before the night is over, cocksucker." Diego playfully threw punches at Benny. "Come on, Manny, let's hit the streets." The two men exited the apartment, leaving Benny to his work.

■

"What's good wit ya, playboy?" Jimmy asked, entering the apartment of his best friend and crime partner, Vince. Jimmy and Vince had been best friends since Jimmy had moved to Manhattan from Red Hook, Brooklyn, when he was fourteen. Back then Vince was running short con, but it didn't take long for Jimmy to turn him on to the art of the stickup.

"Maintaining," Vince said, lounging on the sofa. A freshly rolled blunt dangled between his lips.

"Looks like I came right on time," Jimmy said, smiling

and taking the seat next to Vince. When he smiled, his gold teeth glinted in the morning light.

"Don't you always," Vince teased, lighting the blunt. "What you getting into today?"

"Shit, a paper chase, nigga. You know how I do it. It's hot so you know niggaz on the other side is probably gonna be gambling. I was thinking about taking off a dice game or maybe catching one of them dumb-ass little niggaz slipping again," Jimmy said proudly.

"Damn, J, we just hit them niggaz last night. I don't think we should go in again so soon. Let's ride on some of them niggaz from 141st Street instead," Vince suggested.

"Man, I don't feel like waiting till damn near half the night for them niggaz to get they money up. Nah, I'd rather slump one of them Columbus niggaz again."

Vince momentarily considered it but pushed the idea out of his mind. True, the young boys who hustled under Prince weren't the sharpest knives in the drawer, but Prince wasn't a slouch. If they weren't careful, he might wise up. Now, they might've been able to go at it with Prince and his crew and not catch too much hell, but if Diego butted in, then it would be more than a wrap for the two stickup kids.

"Nah, we ain't gonna do that tonight, Jimmy. Let's get some pussy and get fucked up instead. We can get back at it tomorrow."

"Let me find out your ass is scared?" Jimmy teased Vince. He knew there was nothing sweet about his partner, but he also knew that with enough prodding he could get Vince to come out with him.

"Nigga, you know better than that," Vince said seriously. "I just ain't trying to get greedy with it. We just hit them niggaz last night so you know they're gonna be on point for it. Why you so fucking gung-ho to keep hitting Prince anyway?"

"Cause they got it, and we need it. We can take these niggaz packs and sell them shits to them Dominican niggaz on 84th Street for less than street value."

Jimmy was sincere on what he planned to do with the drugs they stole from Prince, but he wasn't completely truthful about his reasons. Jimmy had been fucking with this girl from the other side of the projects and found himself smitten with her. She stripped at this club in the Bronx, but her beauty and down-to-earth personality made him look past her career choice. He finally thought that she was a chick he could fuck with like that, until he found out she and Daddy-O had an ongoing thing. It wasn't the fact that she was fucking Daddy-O that pissed him off, but the fact that she was fucking him for paper. He hated Daddy-O for it and was hell-bent on making him suffer.

"J, you know you my nigga, can't get no bigger, but this ain't the wisest plan you've ever come up with. We're cutting the shit too close," Vince said.

Jimmy thought on it for a minute. "You're right, my dude. It's just the thought of all that paper made me kinda crazy for a second. The rest of these niggaz don't pay as well as Prince's boys."

"I be knowing, kid. Between what we took off Gene and that other lame mutha fucka, we had like three stacks. Don't even trip off that shit though. Go see ya young bitch and leave that shit for another day. They'll still be selling crack tomorrow."

"Fo sho." Jimmy gave Vince a pound. "I'm 'bout to go see my bitch."

"That's what I'm talking about, son. Shit, I'm gonna call a bitch and see about getting my freak on too. Call me if you wanna make it a double date!" Jimmy said.

"That's a bet," Jimmy assured him as he left the apartment. No sooner than the door closed behind him, he was scheming. To Jimmy, Prince and his crew were sweet and ripe for the plucking. If his man didn't want in on the lick, that just meant he didn't have to split the take.

CHAPTER 7

The Sugar Shack was an out-of-the-way spot located on 139th Street and 8th Avenue in Harlem. It wasn't as glitzy as some of the more established nightspots in Manhattan, but you could go there and get your drink on or enjoy a meal.

By the time Daddy-O and Prince got to the spot, there were already some heads from the projects in the building helping Sharon celebrate her twenty-first. Keisha and her girls were in the joint, drinking and cussing like dudes. Though they were easy on the eyes, these were some of the roughest broads in the hood.

Prince and Daddy-O had traded in their street ware and dressed for the evening. Daddy-O was wearing a white, short-sleeved button-up with sky blue jeans and white and blue Delta Force Nikes. Prince didn't go button-up, but he had on a crisp black T-shirt, dark blue Enyce jeans, and low-cut black Timberland chuckers. His White Sox fitted hat was pulled so low over his face that you could barely see his eyes.

A few dudes who knew the duo nodded and raised drinks in their direction. Keisha and her crew, who appeared to be tipsy, shouted them out from across the room. Prince scoffed at the attention but didn't take it personal. That's just how Keisha was. Prince and Daddy-O treated them to a bottle of champagne but didn't spend too much time at their table. There were some fine females in the joint that night, and the last thing they needed was the neighborhood girls cramping their style.

Daddy-O was having a ball eye-fucking damn near every woman who passed him. Prince on the other hand seemed withdrawn. Though Prince was trying to act like everything was good, Daddy-O knew his friend better than that. Diego had wounded his pride. Prince had made Diego tons of money over the last few years, and his loyalty was never a question. He'd gone harder for Diego than his own inner circle, but the deeds seemed to go unnoticed. Everyone knew that Prince was more than qualified to run his own show, but he needed Diego's backing to solidify it. A stand-up dude would've given Prince his blessing as long as he was still seeing a piece of the pie, but Diego was proving time and again that the age of the real nigga was dying out. He didn't want peers, he wanted sons.

"You still tripping off that shit, son?" Daddy-O nudged him, causing some of Prince's drink to splash on the bar.

"Nah, I'm good," Prince grumbled.

"Yo, that nigga Diego be on some real bullshit. You brought the projects back to life, and he won't even let you reap the benefits of it."

"It's all good, Daddy."

"Nah, it ain't all good, Prince. We've been putting in work for that greedy spic since we were kids and don't ever get a shred of fucking gratitude."

"The man is just protecting his territory," Prince tried to convince Daddy-O as well as himself.

"Something has got to give," Daddy-O said, ordering two more shots.

"I hear that shit, man, but what? We gotta find a way to do our own thing without bringing them Germans down on our asses. Give me some time, and I'll come up with something."

"I know you will." Daddy-O slapped him on the back. "Whatever you wanna do, I'm wit you, my dude." Daddy-O raised one of the shots the waitress had sat down on the bar and slid the other one to Prince. "From the womb to the tomb, my nigga."

"Cradle to the grave, baby boy." Prince raised his glass. The two men downed their shots and slammed the empty glasses on the bar.

■

Back in the projects, the mood wasn't quite as light. Things had been tense since the string of recent robberies, and no one had yet to come up with an answer as to who was behind them. But Sticks had an idea, and this was why Jay was standing alone in the very same parking lot Gene had gotten robbed in.

Jay was pissed when Sticks had hatched his plan, making him the bait for the would-be robbers. He didn't like being used as a pawn, but he wasn't stupid enough to argue with Sticks. Though he was the less violent of the twins, he had heard rumors about Sticks's methods of dealing with people. The thought alone made him cringe.

"Let me get two," a crackhead said, approaching Jay. Jay nodded and dipped into the crack of his ass, where he kept his stash. He dug into the Ziploc and filled the crackhead's order. The crackhead thanked him and disappeared across the parking lot.

As Jay watched the crackhead shamble through the project, he thought he saw movement along the side of 825. His heart immediately began to race as he scrambled under the car, where he had a small .22 stashed. By the time he came up holding the gun, he found himself aiming at a raggedy umbrella that was blowing in the warm breeze. Jay exhaled and lowered the gun. When he turned to put the gun back in its hiding place, he found himself looking down the barrel of a Beretta.

"What the fuck was you gonna do with that?" Jimmy asked from behind his ski mask.

Jay opened his mouth, but no sound came out. His eyes darted around in the hopes that a member of his team was close by, but to his dismay he was alone. He didn't know how the masked man had crept up on him like that, but he prayed that he would live long enough to find out.

"Run it, nigga. I want the pack, the money, and that cheap-ass chain," Jimmy said, tapping the gold cross that Jay wore with the barrel of his gun.

"You know who you robbing, nigga?" Jay snarled. In answer to his question, Jimmy smashed the butt of his gun into Jay's nose, breaking it. Jay was down and crying, but it didn't slate Jimmy's rage.

"You think I give a fuck about yo faggot-ass team? Run yo shit or get dumped on, bitch!" Jimmy snatched Jay's pants down and retrieved the package of crack that was tucked between his ass cheeks. He held it between two fingers and made a face. "Nasty-ass niggaz," he kicked Jay in his exposed ass. Jimmy dipped through the projects grinning, but the grin melted away when a bullet whizzed past his ear and struck the fence in front of him.

■

Two hours and four drinks later, the men had forgotten about Diego and focused on getting drunk and laid. The action in the Sugar Shack had started to pick up, and the women were rolling in by the score.

Prince turned around to go to the bathroom and bumped into a young lady who was trying to squeeze her way back to her friends. When they collided her Midori Sour splashed all over Prince's black T-shirt. He started to bark on her, but when his eyes met her face he found himself speechless.

Shorty was the baddest thing he had seen in a long time. At five-five with a honey complexion and long black hair, she was definitely giving the other women in the room something to think about.

"Oh, I'm so sorry," she said, looking at the large wet spot on Prince's T-shirt.

"Nah, that's my bad. I should've been paying attention," Prince said, shaking the excess liquid off his shirt. "Let me replace that for you," he said, nodding at her now half-empty glass.

"You don't have to do that," she said, continuing through the crowd. Prince grabbed her arm before she could scurry off.

"I think it's only right, seeing how I knocked that one over," he insisted, smiling at her.

Marisol looked at the hand clutching her arm and scrunched her face as if it was something vulgar. She started to bark on him for touching her uninvited, but there was

76

something about his rich chocolate skin and breathtaking smile that made her hesitate. "You're awful touchy for a stranger," she said.

"My fault, ma, but it's not everyday that a man comes face to face with a goddess, and I was just trying to prolong the moment."

"Well, thank you for the compliment, but I think we've prolonged the moment long enough. My girls are waiting for me," she said, turning to walk away.

"At least let me replace your drink," Prince tried one more time.

Her face said that she was considering it, but her mouth said otherwise. "I don't let strange men buy me drinks, sorry, poppy." She tried to walk off one more time only to have Prince stop her yet again.

"My name ain't poppy."

"Excuse you?" she looked at him.

"I said, my name ain't poppy. It's Prince," he said as if his name should've meant something to her and everyone else in the room.

The girl gave the cocky young man the once-over. He was dressed very plainly in a black T-shirt and blue jeans, hardly the type of cat that she was used to dealing with, but Prince was very handsome. His smooth skin looked like a freshly dipped chocolate bar under the dim lights. Yeah, he definitely had it going on, but she wasn't about to tell him that.

"Okay, Prince," she said, letting his name roll sexily off her tongue.

"You got a name, ma?"

She thought on it for a minute before answering. "Marisol."

"Beautiful," he whispered.

"My name?" she asked.

"Nah, you."

"Thank you," she said, with color flushing her cheeks.

"So, now that we're not strangers anymore, why don't you sit down and have a drink?"

She smiled, showing perfect white teeth. "Sounds good, Prince, but I can't leave my team like that," she said, motioning toward one of the tables in the rear of the lounge where there were three stunning sets of eyes watching the exchange closely. Marisol's friends were all sexy-ass shades of brown with silky hair.

"Damn, if that's ya team we need to be over there with y'all," Daddy-O said. He winked at one of the girls, causing her to giggle and whisper something to the other two.

Prince called the bartender over and whispered something in her ear before turning back to Marisol. "Tell you what, how 'bout if we come join y'all?"

Marisol gave him a playful smile. Her eyes said come on, but her mouth said, "Hold on a second, let me see what my girls wanna do." Marisol told him she would return and sauntered back to the table where her girls were sitting. Feeling

Prince's eyes still on her, she made it a point to throw her ass extra hard when she walked.

Daddy-O let out a whistle. "That is one bad bitch!"

"You ain't never lied about that," Prince dapped him up and the two men laughed.

Sticks wanted to slap the shit out of Danny for fucking up a perfectly laid trap. Pam, who lived on the first floor of 845, had called his cell phone to tell him that Jay was being robbed, as he expected. He had given her two hundred dollars worth of crack just to sit by the window and watch for anything funny. Sure enough, the greedy-ass stickup kid was back. They were supposed to creep on the kid while he was robbing Jay and air his ass out. It was a perfect plan, but Danny had fucked it up by firing too early. Now they found themselves in a running firefight.

When the shot hit the fence, Sticks expected the masked man to immediately bolt, but he had a surprise for him. Firing in a one-handed grip, the gunman tried to take Sticks and Danny out. Danny dove behind a car and remained there while Sticks wove and dodged through the parking lot.

"Stupid mutha fucka," Sticks cursed under his breath as he narrowly dodged a bullet. He popped from behind the car and let off two shots from his P89. The cannon sounded like thunder as Sticks shot out two car windows, but he missed the masked man, who was now running full out toward Manhattan Avenue.

■

Jimmy burst from the parking lot like he had the devil on his heels. He collided with a neighborhood drunk and fell, scraping his leg something awful. Jimmy fought through the pain and was back on his feet in seconds. His partner had warned him about trying to pull another lick so soon, but he didn't listen, and for his hardheadedness he might not live to tell him he was right. His only hope was to make it to 100th Street where there were some people barbecuing. Sticks was crazy, but not crazy enough to gun him down in front of so many witnesses. Unfortunately, Stone had no such qualms.

BOOM! BOOM! BOOM!

At the sound of gunfire, the grill was quickly abandoned, sending people scattering for cover. Jimmy too, heard the thunderous clap, but didn't register what he was hearing until the slug from the .357 ripped through the muscle and cartilage of his thigh before snapping the bone on impact. The force was so powerful that it flipped Jimmy in the air and dumped him on his back. The pain in Jimmy's thigh was so intense that he just wanted to lay down and fade away, but he couldn't. The fear from what Sticks and Stone would do to him willed strength to his arms as he tried to crawl away.

"Don't dip off just yet, we're just getting started," Stone

taunted, grabbing Jimmy by the back of his hoodie and dragging him. Jimmy tried to bring his gun around only to have Stone kick it from his hand. "Oh, now you wanna pop me, huh?" Stone kicked him viciously in the mouth.

"Chill," Jimmy wheezed through his busted lips.

"Chill? Nah, man, ain't no chill. You trying to take food off my table?" Stone stomped Jimmy's ruined leg.

"For once your ass was on time for something." Sticks smirked as he approached the scene.

"Fuck you, Sticks. You almost let this grease ball mutha fucka get away," Stone shot back. Jimmy's moans broke up their argument and brought them back to the business at hand. "Let's see who we got here," Sticks said, removing Jimmy's mask. When he saw that it was Jimmy, he just shook his head. "I should've known. A'ight, this is what we're gonna do . . ." Sticks was cut off as Jimmy's chest exploded. He turned around furiously and glared at his brother, who was wearing a goofy smirk.

"Ashes to ashes, mutha fucka!" Stone spat on Jimmy's corpse.

"Nigga, you shot him before I got him to squeal on his man!" Sticks shouted.

"Fuck we need him to squeal for when we already know him and Vince is thick as thieves. Who the fuck else could have been robbing our workers with him. All we gotta do is go snatch his ass next."

"Okay genius, so where do we find him?"

"Oh, I hadn't thought of that," Stone admitted. They knew that Vince lived somewhere near the projects, but they didn't know exactly where.

"Bring yo stupid ass on, man," Sticks told his twin as he disappeared back into the projects.

■

Prince and Daddy-O hit it off with Marisol's crew immediately. Lizzie seemed to take a liking to Daddy-O from the gate, so they wound up pairing off. Prince and Marisol laughed as their two drunken-ass friends hit the dance floor and were busting their two-step. Feeling like the odd ladies out, Marcy and Connie excused themselves from the table, leaving Prince and Marisol to get acquainted.

Two empty bottles of champagne sat on their table, with the third halfway there. Prince and Daddy-O had sprung for the first two, and to their surprise Marisol had copped the third. Prince tried to be chivalrous about it, but Marisol wasn't trying to hear it. She wanted to make it clear from the gate that she held her own and didn't need a man to do anything for her. He had no choice but to respect it.

The constant flow of champagne had them both feeling talkative. Prince told her a little bit about himself and his upbringing. She figured him for a street cat, but he downplayed it, claiming that he only moved a few pieces here and there. Marisol told him about herself, without giving away too much. She told him that she worked for her family's restaurant part-time and attended school three days a week. She had originally made the pilgrimage to America from Cuba when she was five years old. She, her mother, and two older brothers had stayed in Miami until their father was caught smuggling drugs and given twenty-years in federal prison. After their family had been broken up, her mother, brother, and she fled to New York.

In turn he revealed to her the events that led him to the lifestyle he had chosen, without incriminating himself or his crew. Prince admitted to Marisol that he made moves here and there, but didn't tell her how deep in the game he was. He was tipsy, not stupid. By the end of the night they felt like they had known each other for years.

"Damn, I've been sitting here running my mouth all night," Marisol looked at her watch. The dim lights caught off the tiny pink diamonds that encircled the face.

"It's all good, I enjoy hearing you speak," he told her.

"Quite the charmer." She patted his hands. "You know what, I wanna propose a toast." she raised her glass. "To good friends and good times."

"Very good times," Prince ran his tongue over his full lips.

"Don't throw the pussy away before you even find out if you're gonna get it," she laughed good naturedly, and clicked glasses with Prince.

CHAPTER 8

It was well after 3:00 A.M., but there were still a sprinkling of people hanging out in the projects. Most of the regular folk had called it a night, giving the hustlers and crackheads free reign over the land. Sticks, Stone, and Danny were posted up around the mouth of the 103rd Street entrance, surveying the Columbus side of the projects. They were having a deep discussion, but all fell silent when a cherry red BMW 528 pulled to a stop directly in front of them. They tried to see who was driving, but all the windows were tinted.

"Who the fuck is that?" Stone whispered to his brother, inching closer to the gun he had stashed in the grass. They had whacked Jimmy, but Vince was still missing. The back door, on the street side popped open and when the passenger emerged, the crew let out a sigh of relief.

Daddy-O stretched and rubbed his gut like he had just

eaten a hardy meal. From the way he teetered, you could tell that he had been drinking. The other rear door opened and Lizzie stepped out, drawing "oh's" from the fellas posted up. She was killing 'em in a pair of black Capris and lace-up sandals that tied around her calves. Daddy-O stepped around to the curb side and gave her a warm hug.

"Don't forget to call me, nigga," she pinched his gut.

"No doubt, ma. If I don't do nothing else I'm gonna call you," he said, drinking her in with his eyes. She kissed him gently on the cheek and went around to the passenger's side, where Prince was stepping out. His eyes too, held a slight twinkle, but it wasn't from the alcohol. Marisol had provided him with good company and conversation, something he didn't get from the girls he fucked within the projects. She was someone he could definitely see himself keeping time with.

"This is your hood, huh?" Marisol rolled the driver's side window as Prince stepped onto the curb.

"Monster Island, the only home I know," Prince said with a smile.

"Why do they call it Monster Island?" Marisol asked.

"I'll tell you the next time I see you," He said, slyly.

"Who said there's gonna be a next time?" she teased.

"Cut that out, ma. You know you're feeling a nigga."

"Umm, hmm. No more than you're feeling me."

"True," he nodded.

"Yo, Prince, who dat?!" Stone shouted. Prince ignored him and turned his attention back to Marisol.

"So, when can I see you again?" he asked.

"You've got the number, use it," she told him.

"I'll do that," he tapped the car door. "So, would it be too much to ask for a kiss?"

"Being that you have to ask, yes," she said, rolling the window partially up, then pausing. "Next time take the initiative." She gave Prince a wink and pulled out into traffic.

"Yo, that was a bad bitch, kid. Who the fuck was that?" Sticks asked.

Prince watched the taillights until they disappeared down Columbus Avenue. "My future wife."

"You know you was wrong for that, Marisol," Lizzie said, peeking through the rear window at Prince, who was standing on the curb smirking.

"Can't make it too easy, can I?" Marisol snickered. "Besides, he'll get his chance."

"You gonna give that buck nigga some pussy ain't you?" Lizzie asked slyly. Marisol gave her a look, but didn't answer. "I always knew you had a thing for chocolate," Lizzie teased.

"He a'ight," Marisol said nonchalantly.

"Bitch, that nigga is fine. You know I love my poppies, but you gotta call a spade a spade, and that spade has got it together!"

"Whatever, ho. Don't act like I ain't see you all up on his man. Shit, I thought y'all was gonna fuck on the dance floor."

"When I felt that snake pressing against my ass, I sure as hell thought about it. Whoever said all fat niggaz had little dicks didn't know Daddy-O!"

"Liz, your ass is crazy!" Marisol said, headed across 125th to the Tri-Borough Bridge.

"So, have you thought about what Felix is gonna say?" Lizzie asked, becoming serious.

Marisol cut her eyes at her. "Like I give a shit about what Felix is gonna say."

"Wow, where did that come from?" Lizzie asked, knowing that her friend was head over heels in love with Felix.

"I'm tired of his shit, Liz. All Felix does is come over, fuck me, and beg for dope. That fool ain't about shit."

"Ah, you're just now figuring out what we've been trying to tell you for the longest. Cano told you not to fuck with him, but you wouldn't listen."

"Liz, I don't need another lecture. I get enough of that shit from Cano."

"How is that sexy-ass brother of yours?"

"He's still in South America. He should be back in another two weeks though, so I'm handling things while he's gone."

"Cano let you into the family business, huh?" Lizzie asked surprised.

"Hardly, when he left I stole two bricks from one of his apartments."

"Girl, you must've fell and bumped ya head! Cano is gonna fuck you up when he finds out," Lizzie said seriously. "Marisol, I don't understand you. Cano spoils you rotten, and you go and steal from him. What the hell were you thinking about?"

Marisol banged her fist against the steering wheel. "I don't know, Liz. This was my father's business and Cano acts like he's king shit. He says he keeps me away to protect me, but that's just an excuse for him to try and run my life. I'm twenty-one years old, and he still treats me like a kid. I just wanted to show him that I can handle it."

"Marisol," Lizzie began, flashing a hint of accent. "You're my girl, so you know I'm gonna keep it gangsta with you. I know you came up around that shit all your life, but drugs are a very serious business, especially heroin. You're playing with fire, and you're gonna fuck around and get burnt."

"You don't think I know that?" Marisol said with an edge to her voice. "Sorry, I didn't mean to snap. Look, what's done is done, and I can't change that. All I can do now is hope that Cano doesn't get too mad about the money I lost."

"And you lost money?" Lizzie asked in disbelief. "How did you manage to fuck that up?"

"I didn't fuck anything up, that asshole Felix did."

Lizzie slapped herself on the forehead. "Marisol, tell me you didn't give that man your brother's drugs?"

"He works for him, so it seemed like the logical thing," she reasoned.

"Yes, as a soldier. Cano kept him at that level because he's a fuck-up, Marisol. Everyone knows that."

"Felix is not a fuck-up!" Marisol defended.

"If it walks like a duck."

Marisol sighed. "I figured he could flip the work and make us some money. Then when Cano came back, I'd have his money and prove to him that I knew how to handle myself and that Felix wasn't a *fuck-up*, as you call him."

Lizzie just shook her head. Marisol had done some dumb things since they'd known each other but never this dumb. Instead of running how wrong she was into the ground, she decided to try and figure out how to help Marisol out of it. "Okay, how much does he owe so far?"

Marisol thought on it for a minute. "Well, so far I've given him about a half a kilo at eighty grand, street value. For a whole one, you do the math."

"Jesus, Marisol, he's into Cano for at least forty grand! Cano is gonna shit a brick. What are you gonna do?"

"Honestly, I don't know, but I've got two weeks to figure it out."

CHAPTER 9

Over the next few days, the heat seemed to increase, if that was at all possible. There had even been a report of a young kid falling out from trying to drink liquor in the swelter. Prince slouched on the benches closest to 865 wearing a tank top and denim shorts. A thin film of sweat had formed over his muscular arms, adding sheen to his almost perfectly dark complexion. Though he was polishing off his second bottle of water in ten minutes, his blood still felt like it was boiling.

"Fuck it's hot!" Daddy-O said, running a hand towel over his sweat-soaked face. His white T-shirt was so saturated that he had to hang it on the gate to dry.

"They said it's gonna be like this all week," Danny said. He was dressed in an oversized Los Angeles Lakers basketball jersey and the throw-back purple and yellow Converse.

"Shit, once I finish up these last few packs, I'm going up to the crib to get up in some pussy."

"Pussy, nigga it's too hot to fuck!" Daddy-O said.

"It ain't never too hot to fuck," Danny shot back.

"Speaking of fucking," Daddy-O turned to Prince. "Son, whatever happened with you and that chick Marisol?"

"Oh, we cool," Prince said as if that should've been enough.

"Cool? Nigga, you ain't try to punch them guts in yet?"

Prince just shook his head, not wanting the whole projects in his business. Actually they had been getting more acquainted than he let on. While Daddy-O slept his hangover off the other morning, he was on the phone with Marisol. He claimed that he was just calling to see if she had made it home okay, but in all actuality he just needed to hear her voice. They had chatted on the phone for hours and only hung up with the promise of meeting up the same evening. Under the cover of darkness and without either of their friends knowing, Prince and Marisol shared a romantic evening consisting of dinner and a movie, but no sex.

"Man, you better quit playing and tap that ass before someone else beats you to the punch," Daddy-O said.

"That ain't my girl. She can do what she wants, kid," Prince said.

"Speaking of do, what does that chick do?" Danny asked. "That BMW was fly as hell!"

"Her family owns some fancy Spanish restaurant in

Queens, so she works there when she doesn't have classes," Prince informed him.

"That must be some fucking restaurant for her to be pushing a beamer," Danny said.

Prince had actually thought about it. Marisol had told him that it was a gift from her brother, but he wasn't sure if he believed it. The night he met Marisol, he peeped her style. Her gear was on point, and he knew the Louis sandals she had on had cost a grip because he had been with Diego when he had copped a pair for one of his chicks. Maybe she had a sugar daddy somewhere, or maybe she was selling ass to keep up her high-end lifestyle, but one thing he was sure of was that she wasn't getting it like that from working part-time in a restaurant.

"Nigga, you hear me talking to you?" Daddy-O asked, snapping Prince out of his daze.

"Huh?"

"I said Danny and them niggaz is almost finished with the fifty grams, and we need to re-up," Daddy-O repeated. "Son, where is your head at?"

"My fault, kid, I was caught up in the moment."

"Probably caught up thinking about Marisol," Daddy-O teased him.

He was half right. True, Prince had thought of Marisol often, but she wasn't what had him distracted. Ever since he had spoken with Scatter, he couldn't help but to think about the advantages of dealing heroin. The sweet poison would help him kill two birds with one stone. Setting up a dope shop would allow him to get out from under Diego's thumb, without interfering with his crack money so it could be an amicable split. But the problem still remained that he didn't have a heroin connect. There were cats he could holla at and probably score some, but it would be the same watered down bullshit that Scatter was talking about. He needed that head-banger.

"So what you wanna do? You gonna go see Diego or you want me to do it?" Daddy-O asked, still oblivious as to what was on his partner's mind.

Prince thought on it for a minute. The show had to go on, but he didn't feel like seeing Diego's face at the moment. "Nah, you go see him. I got a move to make right quick," Prince said, heading out of the projects. He valued the company of his team, but at the moment he needed to be away from the game so he could sort some things out in his head.

CHAPTER 10

"**Y**ou know I was surprised to hear from you," Marisol said, running her finger along the line of Prince's chest.

"Shit, I was surprised I called. I ain't want you getting gassed up thinking I was all on your shit." He kissed her forehead.

"And what would've given me that idea?" she teased.

Marisol knew that she was going to give Prince some pussy from the moment she met him, but hadn't planned on doing it so soon. She was pleasantly surprised when Prince had called her that afternoon. He asked if they could hang out, but she told him she had to study. Both of them felt the urge to see each other, so they compromised and she invited him over for an early dinner.

He showed up on her doorstep with a bottle of champagne, rocking a crisp white T-shirt, and an LA Dodgers fitted. The way he wore his hat cocked on his head gave him an air of confidence that made her moist in her secret places. After they devoured the fried chicken and rice that she had whipped up, the two lovers sipped champagne and blew trees while they watched the first season of *The Wire* on DVD, which as it turned out was both their favorite show. Prince related to it because the characters went through the same shit that he did on the day-to-day basis. Marisol listened intently as he philosophized about what it meant to be truly married to the game. Not only was this man ruggedly handsome but he had a brilliant mind, which only had her more open.

By about the third episode, they had engaged in a lip lock that had them both gasping for air. His strong, yet gentle hands explored her body, sending chills all the way down to her toes. Her mouth tried to say no, but her body wouldn't listen as she shuddered under his touch. In record time, Marisol had stripped down to nothing but her thong. Prince ran his tongue down the center of her breasts, flicking across her hardened nipples. He continued his oral exploration across her belly, stopping briefly around her navel. Marisol got so wet that it would be a wrap for her thong even if they didn't fuck.

When he got down near her pussy, he teased it through her thong with his tongue. She tried to force his head down, but he slapped her hands away. It was clear that it was his show, and she was just a spectator. Pulling her thong to the side, he began to lap at her clit, causing her to hiss. Prince's cell phone rang, but Marisol tossed it across the room before he could even think about answering it. There was no way in the hell one of his boys or another bitch was gonna fuck this up for her. Prince's tongue danced over and around her pussy before he dipped it inside her. The tip of it felt like a hot spear stabbing against her walls. Marisol was so grossed with Prince's tongue lashing that she tore his T-shirt clean off his back. Just when she thought it couldn't get any better, he flipped her on her stomach and repeated the process in her ass. It was the first time a man had ever tossed her salad, and she was damn near climbing the walls.

Marisol was on her stomach with her ass cocked in the air, flexing her cheeks in time with his tongue. Cum soaked her inner thighs and his chin, but he didn't seem to mind as he munched her like a $2.99 buffet. When Prince balanced himself on his arms and entered her from behind, Marisol saw flashes of light. Prince started off with slow strokes, bringing the light flashes every time he pumped. In record time Marisol had cum, lubricating her pussy and allowing him to dig deeper into her guts.

Prince knew that he had a big dick, and from the way Marisol tensed up so did she. She was wet as hell already, but he still had a hard time getting in. Once Marisol had cum, it was easier for Prince to get in and do his thing. He hit her with long strokes at first then rapid short ones. He switched speeds on her back and forth until she didn't know whether she was coming or going. To say that Marisol had some good pussy would've been an understatement. They say that there are seven wonders in the world, but Marisol's pussy surely had to be the eighth.

Tired of being the passenger, Marisol decided to take the wheel. She climbed out from under Prince and pushed him on his back. Her large breasts clapped softly together as she threw her leg across Prince to straddle him. The moment his dick slipped in she regretted it. It felt like if she slid any further down it would burst from her mouth. After a few attempts she was able to find a comfortable position and began to ride Prince. She started off slow at first, but once the pain turned to pleasure, she went for broke. After about forty minutes, Prince finally came, and they lay in the middle of her living room carpet reflecting on what had just happened.

■

"So, where's your boy?" Diego asked Daddy-O, who was standing in the kitchen of the armory.

Daddy-O shrugged. "Said he had something to do, so he sent me to pick up the work."

The look on Diego's face said that he didn't believe him, but it was the truth as Daddy-O knew it. "Yeah, I ain't seen a lot of Prince since the night Manny whipped E's punk ass. He ain't even taking my phone calls. Is he still stunting what happened to his man?"

"Nah, you know Prince understands the business," Daddy-O said.

"Does he? Anyhow, what's going on in the hood? I heard somebody got dropped in the parking lot. You know anything about that?"

"Nah, I heard about it, but it wasn't us," Daddy-O lied. Diego clasped his hands behind his back and moved slowly toward Daddy-O. Daddy-O's heart began to pound in his chest, but he held fast.

"You know," Diego leaned in to whisper, "when niggaz die in my hood, especially without my say so, it brings heat. And when the hood is hot I lose money. Whoever was behind that body cost me a grip, and I'm not happy about it. Now, I know you say you don't know nothing about it, but being that you're out there I'm sure you're gonna hear something about it."

"Yo, D . . ."

Diego raised his hand for silence. "Daddy-O, I don't even wanna hear it. You niggaz is supposed to be minding my candy shop, so how the fuck you gonna tell me that you don't know what's going on at all times? You know what, I don't even know why I'm talking to you. Tell that little mutha fucka Prince to get with me ASAP. If he don't get with me, Manny is gonna get with him," he motioned to the killer. "We clear on that, fam?"

"Crystal."

■

Prince had finally managed to gather the strength to go over and recover his cell phone. There was a message from a chick he had met the week before on the block. She was a chicken head from 110th with a mean head game and a shot of so-so pussy. He glanced over at Marisol, who was lying on the floor with one thick thigh slung on the couch. He chuckled ironically as he deleted the message. There were two on there from Daddy-O telling him that Diego was looking for him, and he wasn't a happy camper. The last and most intense one was from Diego himself.

Though Diego didn't say on the phone, Prince knew why he was so anxious to speak with him. Prince had allowed his men to murder someone on Diego's turf without permission. Jimmy and Vince had violated and Prince made a judgment call. Had he ran it past Diego there was no doubt that he would've OK'd the hit, but Prince hadn't asked and that bruised Diego's ego. What was done was done and there was no undoing it, and if given the choice he would've done it again. Diego wasn't in the trenches, so he could go fuck himself if he didn't like how Prince did things.

"Fuck you too," Prince said as he deleted the message.

"Who was that, ya girl?" Marisol called from behind him. She had flipped over onto her stomach as her chin was resting on the backs of her hands.

"Nah, that was just some hood bullshit. I'll figure out

how to deal with it when I get back to the block," Prince told her. She could tell from the look on his face that something was troubling him.

"Anything I can do to help?" she asked, sincerely.

"Not unless you've got a good connect," he joked. Something flashed across Marisol's eyes that made him think he had offended her. "Sorry, it was a bad joke."

Marisol scooted closer to Prince and rested her head in his lap. Just having her that close to him drained some of the tension that had built in his gut. He looked down at her and she was more beautiful to him, as if it was even possible. *I'm gonna have to stop fucking with this bitch before I find myself sprung*, he thought to himself.

"Prince," she said, reaching behind her head to stroke his dick through his boxers. "Why don't you stop bullshitting me and tell me what's going down?"

The look Marisol was giving Prince told him that she read more into him than he would've liked. "You don't miss much, do you?"

"Not really," she said seriously. "But listen, if I'm over-stepping my bounds I understand, and we ain't gotta talk about it."

Marisol kept her face innocent, but little did Prince know she already had the 411 on him. Using some of her family's contacts, she had done some research on Mr. Prince Jones. She found out that he was more than just the small-time hustler that he made himself out to be. According to her people he was the right arm of a greedy coke baron named Diego on the Westside. This was part of the reason that she had slept with him. Sure, she dug the hell out of Prince, but she also saw him as a potential solution to her problem. Being seasoned to the game since she was a kid, she knew better than to expose her hand before it was time.

Prince looked at her beautiful face and felt totally at ease. He wasn't stupid enough to tell Marisol too much, but he was comfortable sharing a little of what ailed him. He went on to tell her about his tenure under this cat, whom he refused to mention by name. He expressed to Marisol his yearning to become more than just the next man's lieutenant, but Diego stunted his growth. Marisol kept her face neutral and tried to look surprised on cue, and Prince was none the wiser.

"Damn," was all she said after his story was done.

"Damn is right. I mean, I feel like I owe this nigga, but at the same time I wanna do me. I got a few niggaz that love me like I love them, but love don't get good coke. Diego got that shit on smash."

Marisol thought on it for a minute. She knew it was a gamble, but she needed to get out of the shit she was in. "Well, what if you didn't sell coke?"

Prince gave her a crazy look. "Marisol, no disrespect to you, but if you're about to give me one of those square-up and get a job speeches then save it, cause I don't wanna hear it. On the real, I'm married to the game and I'm gonna be buried with it. That's just how it is."

Marisol gave him a look that said she wasn't impressed with his little statement. She knew Prince was drawing a line in the sand, but she was more than willing to cross it. "Prince, I ain't ya moms, so don't get it twisted like I'm trying to tell you what to do. I'm just asking if you be open to selling something else?"

He didn't like where this was going. "Marisol, I don't know what you've got up your sleeve, but I ain't fucking wit you. You can't possibly do anything but make my situation worse. Thanks, but no thanks, ma."

"Hold that thought," she said, getting off the floor.

Marisol trotted naked up the stairs to the second level of the duplex. Prince continued to lie on the ground and ponder his own situation. He was sorry if he had offended Marisol by telling her to butt out, but she couldn't help him. Since the dawn of time, all women had succeeded in doing was complicating the game, and he didn't need that right then. What he needed was a way to get from under Diego's thumb. No sooner than he had the thought, Marisol came back downstairs and tossed a shopping bag at his feet.

"What the hell is this?" he asked, looking at the bag as if he was afraid to touch it.

"You tell me." Marisol grabbed the bottom of the bag and turned it upside down, dumping a neatly wrapped package in his lap. At first Prince mistook it for coke, but as he examined it his eyes got wide with realization.

"What the fuck is this?" he asked. He wasn't asking her to identify it, but asking what she was doing.

"That, my friend, is one kilogram of Mexico's sweetest blow. Street value, eighty-thousand dollars," she said like a professor giving a lecture to students. "Sometimes it goes for more, but this is only seventy-five or eighty percent pure. Still, you could put a five on it and still have a fiend lose his lunch."

"Marisol, where the fuck did you get this?" Prince asked, still not believing what he was holding.

"Doesn't matter where I got it, baby boy. What matters is that we've both got a problem, and this is the way to solve them." Marisol went on to tell Prince her story, doctoring it as she saw fit. She explained to him that she had a partnership with her brother, who was out of the country on business. In her story one of her lieutenants had burned her on some product and that the suppliers would kill her brother if they didn't come up with the money. She felt bad about not giving Prince the whole story, but the ends justified the means. Besides, when it was all said and done, they'd both be so caked up that it wouldn't matter. Cano would see that Marisol was capable of running the business, and Felix would be out of the picture as his lieutenant. In her naïve mind she was helping Prince as well as herself.

"Damn, we could get rich off this shit," Prince said, star struck.

"Exactly my point," she agreed. "Look, you said yourself that Diego is only interested in coke and crack money, so you could go into business for yourself with the dope."

"Yeah, but I don't know shit about dope," he shamefully admitted. A true hustler knew something about most if not all drugs, even if they didn't sell the particular brand. It was a mistake that Prince made a mental note to rectify.

Marisol smiled devilishly. "That's where I come in," Marisol straddled Prince's lap, facing him. "Grab a pen, baby, cause I'm about to give you a crash course in Blow 101."

CHAPTER 11

𝔓rince wasted no time getting back to the projects and calling a meeting with his people. Assembled were Danny, Sticks, Stone, and Jay. No one quite knew what to make of the off-white substance in the Ziploc bag that Prince had laid out for them, but from what he said, it meant paper and that was about all they needed to know.

"Nigga, you kicking some serious shit," Daddy-O said, finishing off a chicken wing. "What the fuck we know about dope?"

"My dude, what did we know about crack when we came on the scene? We learned that shit on the fly," Prince pointed out.

"Son, I heard you could make stupid paper off a brick of that shit," Danny said, eyeing the dope greedily.

"Dawg, we can all get fat off this. The best part is that I got a mainline to it. Real talk, we can finally get out from under Diego with this shit. You niggaz ain't wit that?" he asked his men.

"Nigga, you're my brother, and I'm gonna fuck wit you regardless, but what about Diego?" Daddy-O said.

"Shit, what about him?" Prince said. "Yo, that nigga is only interested in crack money. If we happen do open up wit this dope in our projects he shouldn't have a problem with it. Even if he does, we can work it out for that kinda bread."

"You gonna step to him with it?" Danny asked.

"Not just yet. I wanna see what we're working with and how much we can move before I burn that bridge." Prince knew that Diego was gonna pitch a bitch, but once he found out that Prince was going to give him a cut, he'd get over it. Diego had nothing to do with Prince getting his hands on the heroin, but out of a sense of loyalty Prince planned to give him a tribute. But not until they got their new hustle down to a science.

There was a soft knock at the door, which Prince nodded for Danny to open. Scatter came into the apartment looking like death warmed over, accompanied by his girl/boosting partner, Ebony. Ebony was a chick that might've been fine back in the days, but constant drug use had added ten years to her appearance. She stepped into the apartment but didn't come past the foyer. She looked at the men in the room then turned her eyes away and let her man handle his business.

Scatter walked with a slight hunch and seemed to be suffering from a stomachache. As usual he was dressed in an expensive suit, but it was wrinkled all to hell. His empty shopping bag hung loosely from his arm, as if he was having trouble holding it up. Scat was obviously sick, which was even better for Prince.

"Prince, what it is man? You told my mom you needed to see me right away?" Scatter's stomach was flipping every-way but the right way. He hadn't had a hit all day long, and his monkey was riding him like the devil. He hoped that whatever Prince wanted from him came with a free bag. As if reading his thoughts, Prince flashed him a devilish grin.

"Scatter," Prince began, slowly scooping a small amount of powder out with a playing card. "We got some shit we 'bout to put out there but we need to see what we're working with," Prince shifted the powder on the card from side to side. "Being that ain't none of us got a whole lot of experience with this, we decided to call in a seasoned cat like ya self to tell us if it's proper," he slid the card to the side of the table, where Scatter was barely standing.

Scatter's eyes began to well up as he reached for the card. When he picked it up, his hand shook so bad that he almost dropped it. "Say, you mind if I do up? I'm sick as hell, and I need this to get right to the point, ya dig?"

Prince ignored the uncomfortable looks some of his crew wore and nodded. Before sitting down to the table, Scatter retrieved a dingy glass from the kitchen and filled it with water. Scatter spared a weary glance at Stone before pulling up a chair. From his inside coat pocket he produced a sock that was tied off in a knot at the end. While the others watched intently, Scatter removed his *works* from the sock.

Scatter dipped the needle into the glass and sucked some of the water up into it. As carefully as he could, he squirted some of the water onto the heroin. When the powder started to sizzle into a loose pastelike substance, Scatter dropped a cotton ball on it and drew the dope into the needle. Danny and Stone turned away, but Prince and Daddy-O kept their eyes on Scatter.

It took him several tries, but with his belt locked firmly around his bicep, Scatter was able to find a good vein on the back of his hand and slipped the needle in. A thin wisp of blood snaked up from his hand into the needle and introduced itself to the dope. Once they'd reached an understanding, Scatter pushed on the plunger and began his ride.

Prince had heard stories and seen dope fiends in the thrall, but watching a real heroin addict take that trip was something else. Scatter sat back in the chair with a pleasant smile on his face. His eyes got droopy and his face got goofy all at the same time. Scatter ground his palm against his crotch like he was reliving the sweetest shot of pussy he had ever had.

"Ummm, yeah," Scatter moaned, jacking the needle in his arm. "This shit is alright, man. You know back in my day . . ." Scatter's eyes suddenly got wide. "Sweet Jesus!" was the last thing he said before falling off the chair onto the floor.

"You niggaz still having second thoughts about coming out with this shit?" Prince asked his crew with a smirk.

■

An hour later, Scatter was still in and out of a deep nod. Thankfully he would be okay, but he was currently vacationing on another planet. Ebony hipped them to the fact that the dope was too strong. Prince didn't even think about cutting it before letting Scatter blast off. Luckily for them Ebony knew what they needed to get the dope ready for sale. Prince gave Danny some money and told him to accompany Ebony to the store to pick up what they needed to cut and package the dope. Daddy-O and Stone stayed behind to watch Scatter and oversee the mixing of the dope when Ebony and Danny came back. Unable to put it off any longer, Prince went to see Diego, which disappointed Manny to no end.

"You know how long ago I called you?" Diego said as soon as Prince walked up on the corner.

"My fault, D, I was handling something," Prince said.

"Ooh, you was handling something? Prince, do I look like I give a fuck what you were handling? My man, you blew Jimmy right in front of the building!"

"I know, D, but . . ."

"But, my ass, Prince," Diego cut him off. "Do you know how much money I lost because I had to shut down when that kid got clapped. And don't try to tell me you didn't know anything about it, because it was one of your boys he robbed. Nobody dies in my hood unless I say so!"

Prince composed himself before speaking. "Diego, the boy was out of bounds and I made a judgment call."

"Judgment? Prince, with all the dumb shit that's gone on lately, I'm starting to question your judgment."

"A'ight, man," Prince said, obviously not wanting to hear what Diego had to say.

"Yo, you act like you don't wanna hear what my dude is telling you, Prince?" Manny stepped up.

"I ain't know I was talking to you," Prince shot back.

Manny stepped up so that he and Prince's noses were only inches from each other. "Well, I'm talking to you."

Manny was trying to lay his pressure game down on Prince but it didn't work out quite how he expected it to. Normally anyone Manny confronted would've backed down out of fear of the killer, but Prince surprised him. By the time Manny noticed the rage building in his eyes, Prince had already hit him twice. The combo staggered Manny, but he immediately came back with a right hook of his own. Prince was able to deflect most of the blow with his arm, but Manny's fist still nicked his head. He was thoroughly surprised at the force Manny had in his bony arms, but Prince was hardly a slouch. He had spent many afternoons sparring with Daddy-O in the park, so he had a few tricks of his own to pull out.

He faked right, and when Manny bit he hit him with the left. Manny followed with a right then a left, catching Prince on the chin and on the side of the head. For a moment, Prince's world swam, but he was able to recover just as Manny was charging him. Prince sidestepped the charge and landed a crushing left to the back of Manny's head. The killer tripped over his own feet and fell flat on his face. He looked up at Prince with blood running down his chin and rage in his eyes. It was only Diego jumping between them that stopped Manny from trying to gun Prince down.

"That's enough!" Diego shouted, which surprised everyone because he never raised his voice in public. "What the fuck has gotten into you two niggaz?"

"That's my word; it's a wrap for you!" Manny threatened. He was now pacing but wouldn't cross the barrier that Diego's body had set up.

"Suck my dick, you fucking faggot!" Prince grabbed his crotch for emphasis. Manny's eye jumped and the murmurs that had been floating on the sidelines suddenly quieted down. In the hood, if you told someone to suck your dick, you had better have a gun in your hand. Prince had violated Manny in front of, not only Diego, but the whole corner.

Manny's face became very serious. "Word?" Before anyone saw him move he had drawn his weapon and was bringing it around to aim at Prince. The situation had gotten out of hand, and Diego's control of the situation was slipping. Before he could flex another muscle, something pressed against his neck.

"What's good, my nigga?" Sticks whispered in his ear. He had a long barreled .357 pressed into Manny's neck. Everyone was so engrossed in the fight that no one noticed him in the crowd watching the fight.

"What the fuck do you think you're doing?" Diego barked at Sticks.

Sticks's eyes flashed murder at Diego, but his voice was very neutral. "Diego, I'd never go against you, poppy. All I know is that I seen ya man pull a gun on one of my brothers, so I gotta hold him down. Don't think I wanna do it like this, but ya man gotta lower his joint." Diego was the boss, but there was something in Sticks's tone that told him it was non-negotiable.

"Son, you better pop me now cause I'm sure as hell gonna pop you on the come around," Manny threatened.

"Nigga, you know ain't neither of us long for this world, but I don't mind speeding up the process on your end," Sticks told him.

"Everybody calm the fuck down," Diego said.

"Diego, you already know I'm gonna put these little nig-gaz to sleep so ain't no need to try and protect them," Manny said seriously.

"Manny, hold ya fucking head! You and Prince is both tripping. Sticks," he addressed the youngster. "Let him go, he ain't gonna do nothing."

Sticks weighed his options. It was so out of character for him to pull a gun and not pop off, but he was dealing with a very delicate situation. In time Diego might forgive the fact that he pulled a pistol around him, but if he killed his friend he would have to kill Diego, and none of their lives would be worth shit. Reluctantly, he began to back away from Manny. He was far from foolish, so he kept the gun pressed against the back of his head until he was a respectable distance away. Manny looked like he was about to make a move, but Diego shook his head and he froze.

"Is you little niggaz crazy?!" Diego moved toward Sticks who reflexively took a step back. Though he was still holding his gun, Diego didn't seem to notice. "I should let Manny dump out on the both of y'all asses for that shit."

"Diego, it's over for them niggaz," Manny said, pacing again.

Diego turned to Manny with storm clouds in his eyes. "My dude, I love you like a brother but if you say one more thing, me and you are gonna have an issue. Prince," he turned to the youngster, who had discretely moved to place Diego between himself and the still-armed Manny. "This is what I mean about shit not being correct in your house. You're totally out of order for this shit."

"Diego, this nigga came at me first, and I did what I had to do. I'm a man just like he is," Prince told him.

"But right now you're acting like a fucking street punk!" Diego shot back. "Prince, take a few days off and get your head together. Daddy-O and them can hold this shit down for a minute."

"Diego, this is my block," Prince said sadly.

"Nah, it's my block and you seem to keep forgetting it. Prince, I need stand-up niggaz that ain't gonna crack on some emotional shit and right now you're not showing me that. Now, I see you over there looking all crazy and shit, so whatever you're thinking you need to un-think it. Don't let ya emotions put you in a bad way."

"I hear you," Prince nodded. He was ready to tear Diego's head off, but he had to be cool. If that's how he wanted to play it, then fuck his block. Prince would just devote his time to getting the heroin popping. Granted, it would be a slower hustle, but slow money was always sho money.

■

Leaving Scatter and Ebony under Stone's watchful eye, Danny decided to make a smoke run. He was supposed to be going right up the block and coming back, but of course the youngster had a head like a brick. He ended up bumping into a kid from the hood named Bobby and getting high with him on the benches.

Six or seven months prior, Bobby had gotten busted with crack on him. With him already being on probation he was supposed to get at least ten to twelve months on a violation, and that's only if they couldn't make the other charge stick. After spending well under a year in jail, Bobby was back on the streets.

"Yo, how long you been home, son?" Danny asked, taking deep pulls of the chronic.

"Like a day or two," Bobby said, sipping his 22 oz.

"Man, I thought sure they was gonna dis you for that possession."

"Nah, them niggaz never read me my rights before they questioned me. I got a Jew on the case that beat it up."

"Them Jews know they shit." Danny passed him the blunt.

"They saved my black ass, kid, word." Bobby hit the blunt twice and handed it back to Danny. "So, what y'all niggaz been up to since I was gone?"

"Out here trying to get a dollar, you know how we do," Danny boasted.

"So Prince is still rocking the block for Diego?" Bobby asked curiously.

"Yeah, you know my nigga out here holding it down. On the real, Diego been on some bullshit lately, man. He make a nigga wanna stop fucking with him."

"Man, everybody gotta fuck wit Diego, he holding all the weight, right?"

Danny blew the smoke out. "Yeah, that nigga got them birds, but he ain't the only connect in town."

"Well, I need to get a connect. I'm trying to get my weight up," Bobby said.

"Listen to ya little ass, talking about getting ya weight up and shit," Danny teased him.

"True story, man. My aunt died while I was away and being that she ain't have no kids, she left me the insurance money."

"Say word!"

"Word, Danny. Yo, I'm trying to take some of that and cop a few grams, but you know Diego don't be fucking wit little niggaz. You think Prince will set me out with some coke?"

Danny looked around before leaning in to whisper to Bobby. "Yo, if I put you on to something, you can't open ya mouth about it."

"Danny, you know I ain't no talking-ass nigga. Come on, you knew me since P.S. 163, what's good?"

"A'ight, check it. How much bread you trying to spend?"

"A couple of hundred, maybe a G if the product is right."

"Man, this shit is beyond right. What we holding got niggaz literally throwing up."

"Throwing up? Dude, I ain't never heard of coke so good that it'll make a nigga earl."

"That's cause it ain't coke." For the next ten minutes Danny sat on the bench and explained their whole operation to Bobby while he listened. The way Bobby hung on Danny's every word, you would've thought he was teaching him one of life's great mysteries. Bobby would teach him a lesson, but there would be nothing mysterious about the move he pulled.

CHAPTER 12

Prince and Sticks went back to the spot and gave Daddy-O, Danny, and Stone the rundown. Daddy-O couldn't believe that it had gone down like that, while Danny just looked nervous. Only two members of the crew had been involved in the conflict, but would the whole crew be held accountable?

Sticks and Stone immediately took stock of how many hammers they had to go around. They had a P89, a .357, a 9 mm, and a .40 cal. Four guns between them wouldn't be enough if an all-out conflict happened to jump off, but they were enough to give a nigga second thoughts about fucking with them. Though no threat had been made, it was better to be safe than sorry.

Everyone agreed that until they knew what was up with Diego, they would carry on like business as usual. Daddy-O would be in charge for the time being, and Prince would fo-cus on getting the dope popping.

Scatter was dead nice with his shit. He had cut the dope four times and the shit still made Ebony throw up when she tested it. Once the mixing was done Prince bundled them into packs like they did with the crack they sold for Diego. Some of the dope went into small vials that Danny had scrounged up from somewhere to make testers. Scatter and Ebony were to hit the streets with the testers and reach out to every dope fiend they knew to get the buzz going.

■

While Prince and his crew opened up shop, Killa E was coming out of the criminal court building located at 100 Centre Street. The judge had set his bail at fifty thousand dol-lars, and he was out on bond. The only problem now was he had to pay his grandmother back the five grand for the bond, and that would completely tap his stash out. He dug in his pocket for a cigarette to find that the only one he had left had gotten smashed in his personals. "What the fuck else could go wrong?" he mumbled, just before a bird flew overhead and shit on his shoulder.

The same night that E had gotten his ass kicked by Manny, he went out and got drunk while crying over his lack of respect in the hood. All E wanted to do was make a dollar, but hating-ass niggaz like Diego made it hard. On numerous occasions he had fantasized about running up on Diego and blowing his head off, but it wasn't until that night, after downing two pints of one-fifty-one, that he was able to get up the courage.

He had gone home and gotten his trusty 9 mm and hit the streets in search of Manny. He wasn't sure what he was going to do if he saw him, but by then he planned on the liquor having complete control. After about three hours of coasting and no sign of Manny, he decided to go check his baby's mother. No sooner than he called her, he wished he hadn't. She was kicking some fly shit about how her man was upstairs, and she wasn't trying to give him any pussy. Him being drunk and emotional, he went anyway.

There's a little voice that we call reason which lurks in the backs of our minds. This voice is supposed to be the balance between dumb shit and smart shit. When you listened to it you tended to be good, but when you didn't it always ended poorly, which was the case with E. He ended up getting into a fight with the boyfriend and pulling the gun. He hadn't intended on shooting him, but the gun went off. When the smoke cleared, E was locked up on a gun charge and the boyfriend was recovering from a gunshot wound to the stomach in Saint Luke's Hospital.

E already had an open case from a possession charge he had caught with Knox. He had given the DA a low-level soldier from the Amsterdam side of the projects to get the charge knocked down and the promise of a drug program if he kept his nose clean. The kid was so low on the totem pole that no one would miss him, besides that he was already on the run, so E saw it as he was only speeding up the inevitable. Now, he got popped on an attempted murder charge and all the low-level dealers in the world wouldn't make that go away. The streets were hard enough on him, but in jail he would find himself anyone's meat.

CHAPTER 13

When Prince woke up, it was nearly ten o'clock. He cursed himself for not setting the alarm, knowing full well that he had things to do. After a quick shower and changing clothes, he was in a cab on his way to Queens.

Marisol was so happy to see him that she leapt in his arms as soon as she opened the front door. They kissed each other like it was a battle to see who could steal the other's breath quicker. It was funny how they had just seen each other a few days prior, but they felt like lovers who had been reunited after several years. It was only due to a nosy neighbor clearing his throat that they even realized that they were still going at it in the hallway.

Marisol had no idea why she was falling so hard for this man. Like Felix, Prince was a dealer, but unlike Felix he had the ambition and the ability to go to the top. Speaking of

Felix, she realized she hadn't heard from him in a few days. She had already convinced herself that she could forget about the half kilo that she had given him and would just have to explain it to Cano when he came back, but it wasn't like Felix not to call and be all up in her ass. She began to worry that something had happened to him, but she forgot all about Felix when Prince emptied the contents of the shopping bag onto the table.

Prince had not only moved the dope she gave him, but he brought back straight money. Marisol was so overjoyed at seeing all that money that she decided to show Prince just how much she appreciated it. Dimming the lights she began to perform a little striptease for him. She was dressed in jeans and a sweatshirt but made it look sexy as hell when she stripped out of them. When Marisol was down to her panties and bra, she straddled Prince, facing him.

Prince let out soft moans as she grinded on his lap. Even through his jeans, he could feel the warmth of her. Sliding down very seductively, Marisol knelt between his legs. The first time they had sex she hadn't given him head, so this would be a special treat. She stroked his dick through the jeans first before she pulled it out and dipped it in her mouth. She started off licking around the head then moved down the shaft. To Prince's surprise, Marisol took him into the depths of her throat like an old school vet.

Prince wanted to shout to the heavens when he felt those

soft lips go down his shaft and brush against his balls, but he was too cool for that. Marisol jacked him and sucked him until he felt like he was going to pop, and stopped. She turned around on all fours and cocked her ass in the air and slapped it. A wave rode through her soft flesh making him want to bite her. Slowly, she reached around and started fingering herself for him to see. Marisol dipped her finger in and out of her pussy until a froth began to form.

"You like that, baby?" she asked, looking over her shoulder at him.

"You know I do," he said, stroking himself.

Marisol cocked over a little further and spread her pussy lips with her fingers. "Then come get this pussy and show me you like it."

Prince didn't need a second invitation. He stepped out of his pants so fast that he almost tripped and busted his face on the floor. His dick was so swollen that he thought he would pop off before he even got in the pussy. Like the first time, Marisol was tight, but Prince shoved himself roughly inside her. She whimpered but didn't tell him to stop. Prince proceeded to beat the pussy from the back then flipped her over on her side. He had her legs spread like a V and was working out on her insides.

Surprising him, Marisol shifted her weight and knocked him to the ground landing on top of him, but never letting his dick slip out. She clawed Prince and rained spittle on his chest as she rode him like a prized bronco at a county fair. They switched to several different positions before Prince roared and blew his wad. They lay on the ground in a lover's embrace as sleep took both of them to dreamland, where money rained from the sky.

■

"What you need, son?" Danny asked the base head.

"What you got?" the base head asked, wiping his nose with the back of his hand.

"I got brown and I got white, what you need?"

"Word, you got that brown brown, or that bullshit they sell on 110th?"

Danny looked at him like he was stupid. "Yo, don't ever disrespect my team like that, nigga. We got some shit that'll dump you straight on your ass, my dude. Twenty cash and you good money."

"Twenty dollars?" the base head was outraged at the price. "Y'all ain't got them five spots?"

"Nigga, this ain't the candy store. You know our prices. Ten for the white, twenty for the brown. Either you spending or you wasting my time." Danny was feeling himself. Prince was MIA, Daddy-O had gone to get his hair done, and Sticks was banished from the hood, at least that's what he heard. This made Danny the man in charge by default. Being in a position of power, if even for a little while, always made

Danny feel like the mutha fucking man. Sometimes he would pretend he was Prince or even Diego while he was giving orders to the lesser soldiers.

"A'ight, man," the base head snapped Danny out of his daydream. "Give me one and one, but this shit better be proper." The base head took his drugs and slid back through the projects.

Danny had been killing 'em with the one-and-ones. Daddy-O had told him not to carry both packages around with him at the same time, but Danny's greedy ass wanted to cut the little niggaz out of the hundred dollars that came off the dope packs. He needed all that scratch.

"What it is, young blood?" a man rolled up on Danny. He was an older cat with rich brown hair that had begun to gray around the edges. His face was slender, but it didn't quite have that sunken look that most addicts acquired after they had been using for a long period of time. Between that and relatively clean clothes he had on, you could tell that he hadn't been at it long.

"What's good?" Danny gave the man the once-over. He looked familiar, but Danny couldn't place him, which was unusual because Danny knew all the addicts in the projects, but they had been experiencing an influx of newcomers since they had started slinging dope.

"I'm trying to get right," the man said with a smile. "Let me get five of them," the man held a fifty-dollar bill out, which Danny just stared at.

"Five of what?" Danny asked, faking ignorance.

"Come on, D, stop acting like that. Give me five stones."

"Dude, ain't nothing popping out here," Danny told him.

"Danny, how you gonna act like you don't know me, kid. I came to see you with Scat the other day, remember?"

Danny searched his high-ass brain and thought that the head looked familiar, but he couldn't quite remember if he had seen him or not. Danny reasoned that if he knew Scatter he had to be an addict, so he served him.

"Yo, you know we got that blow too," Danny volunteered.

"Say word?" the man's eyes lit up. "Shit, I ain't had a shot of good dope in a minute," the man fished a twenty out of his pocket. "Let me get one." Danny fished a loose bag of dope from his pocket and handed it to the man. The man slit his eyes and handed it back. "Danny, I'm spending seventy-cash with you, you can't do no better than this little-ass bag?"

"Nigga, this ain't the fish market!" Danny barked.

"Don't take it like that, D. All I'm saying is that I'm gonna have to share this with my lady so give me a nice one. She get her check today so you know we gonna come back and spend some paper with you." The man enticed him.

Danny was about to tell him to piss off, but the promise of more money changed his mind. "Hold on, son," Danny turned his back to the addict and dipped his hand down the front of his pants. Though the addict couldn't see what he was doing, the white cat snapping pictures of him from across the street could.

"Good looking out," the addict said, accepting the new, slightly larger bag of dope. He had only been sent to cop rocks, but the knowledge that Diego now had dope on the streets was an added bonus. "I'll bring my wife through to see you later on tonight."

"Do that," Danny said, sitting on the bench. He thumbed through the bills in his pocket, never noticing a smear of red lipstick on a wayward fifty, and smiled to himself. All in all, he had run through ten bundles of crack and a half bundle of dope. By the time he stepped off later on, his PC was going to be looking lovely.

He placed a quick call to a jump-off by the name of Nina who lived on the Amsterdam side of the projects. She was a sexy little bitch that would get down if the money and the mood was right. She knew Danny and his crew were now the niggaz to see, so he was sure to have a good time with her. After confirming that she was with some late-night action, Danny decided to hit the liquor store for a taste.

Danny bopped through the courtyard like he was Diego himself, greeting the little niggaz on the block. His cool-ass stroll had carried him almost to the Avenue when an Impala came speeding through from the direction of Manhattan Avenue. Danny tried to burn it but his sagging pants tripped him up. The two plainclothed officers that were coming on foot from Columbus grabbed Danny's little ass up and slammed him on the ground.

"What's up, Danny?" an officer wearing a bent Yankee hat smirked as he cuffed Danny's hands roughly behind his back.

"Get the fuck off me. I didn't do nothing!"

"Then what'd you run for?" A second cop sporting a buzz cut sifted through Danny's pockets. He only found loose bags of crack and heroin, but it was enough to take Danny off the streets for a few hours. When he dug into Danny's pants and found the two baggies of crack and heroin, he quadrupled the number in his head. "Well what do we have here?" He tossed the baggie containing the heroin to his partner.

"Looks like you boys done came up." Yankee cap showed Danny the baggie of heroin.

"That's not mine!" Danny said nervously.

"Sure it ain't." Yankee cap laughed as he pulled Danny to his feet by his elbow. "You have the right to remain silent. Anything you say can and will be used against you. . . ." The officer read Danny his rights, but Danny couldn't hear anything over the beating of his own heart. This wasn't his first time being taken to the precinct, but from what they had caught him with it would be his first time going to jail. Danny had heard all the dark accounts of the things that went on within the various buildings of Rikers Island, and he feared that he was about to see how close to the truth they were.

■

Prince had a horrible nightmare that night. He dreamt that he was in the projects again about to go at it with Manny. He wasn't quite sure how it happened, but somehow Manny got the drop on him and he ended up on his back. Manny wore a devilish grin as he pointed an impossibly long gun at Prince. Manny tapped the gun against Prince's forehead and whispered, "Wake up, cocksucker."

Prince awoke with a start. At first he was disoriented, but when his eyes were able to focus he remembered that he was at Marisol's. But the person standing over him wasn't his boo.

The man who hovered over Prince was about six feet with a thin goatee. His hair was faded on the side and gelled into curls on the top. He wore a pleasant smile, but there was nothing pleasant about the Desert Eagle that he was pointing at Prince.

Prince felt all the color drain from his face, which was quite a task considering how dark he was. He had his hammer with him, but he had slid it under the couch when he and Marisol started going at it. Even if he was fortunate enough to take out the man standing over him, the other one posted by the door with a shotgun would've surely finished him. Of all the ways Prince imagined himself dying, ass naked in the crib of a bad bitch wasn't one of them.

"So," the man began in a heavy accent. "You're the little mutha fucka that's been stealing my heroin? Well, I'm gonna show you what the fuck we do to thieves."

CHAPTER 14

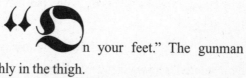n your feet." The gunman kicked him roughly in the thigh.

"Yo, my dude, I don't know nothing about no . . ." Before Prince could finish his sentence the gunman slapped him roughly across the face.

"Negrito, I didn't tell you to talk; I told you to get the fuck up!"

"A'ight, chill." Prince struggled to his feet. He touched his lip, and his fingers came away bloody. Prince tried to reach for his clothes, but when the man placed the Desert Eagle to his ribs he froze.

"Nah, poppy, you won't be needing those," the man grinned at him. From his pocket he produced a pair of hand-cuffs. "Put those on, poppy." Seeing that Prince was hesitant, the gunman pointed the gun at his head. "We can do this the easy way or the hard way." Prince did as he was told. "Good, now bring ya skinny ass on. Somebody wants to meet you." He motioned toward the door with the gun.

It would be embarrassing as hell to walk the streets naked, but it was better than being found dead that way. He would do as he was told until he came up with an escape plan. All of a sudden it dawned on him that Marisol was nowhere to be found. Panic instantly set in. What if the gunmen had her tied up somewhere?

"Where's Marisol?" he blurted out. He didn't even know why he cared when it was probably her that set him up in the first place.

"Oh, you'll be with her soon enough, poppy," the gunman taunted. The way he kept calling Prince *poppy* reminded him of Diego, which only made him hate the man more. Hell, the cats with the guns were probably Diego's people. He swore if he got out of the situation alive, he was going to murder all the of the Hispanics just off GP.

The walk out of Marisol's building was embarrassing as hell. People were looking and pointing, but the gunman didn't seem to notice as he strolled casually to a Navigator that was idling near the curb. The man who had been standing by the door got in the front passenger's seat while the gunman motioned for him to get in the back. When he climbed in the truck, he was surprised to see Marisol, fully dressed and unharmed.

"Oh, baby," she threw her arms around him. "Are you

okay?" Prince just glared at her hatefully. "Baby, I swear on everything I love I didn't have anything to do with this. Cano," she turned to the gunman who had climbed in the back on the other side of her. "You could've at least let him put some clothes on!" Hearing Marisol call him by name meant that she knew him, which made it a no-brainer who Prince planned to kill first.

Prince was tired of playing. It was obvious that he was going to die, and if this was the case he would do it on his feet. "Man, fuck this double-crossing bitch and fuck you!" he said, looking Cano square in the eyes.

With an enraged snarl, Cano leapt across Marisol, who tried to restrain him but just ended up getting pinned under his weight, and dug the barrel of his gun deep into Prince's cheek. "You piece of shit, you steal my dope and then disrespect me? The only reason I'm not gonna push ya shit back is because I want my fucking money and this is a new truck. You know how hard it is to get blood off suede?" He motioned toward the ceiling.

"Man, I tried to tell you I didn't take no dope!" Prince declared.

"Cano . . ."

"No, Marisol!" he snapped. "You will not whine your way out of this one. You wanna run with the big dogs then you gotta respect the rules. Now, if either of you say one more word I'm gonna shoot this piece of shit," he threatened, cocking the gun and pointing it at Prince's head.

My God in heaven, what has my dick gotten me into? Prince thought to himself.

◼

Just as Prince had instructed him, Daddy-O did business as though nothing was wrong. He had seen Diego that day in front of the store with Oscar and Manny. Diego had struck up a conversation with him, trying to see where Daddy-O's head was at, but Prince's partner in crime was unreadable. He admitted to Diego that he had heard about what happened between Prince and Manny, but his stand on it was that he was about a dollar and the situation with Manny would blow over. Diego told Daddy-O what time he would send someone around to drop off more product and pick up the money, and Daddy-O was on his way.

Daddy-O had tried to call Prince to put him up on the conversation, but he didn't answer his cell. Prince was a nigga that never turned his cell off, but that was before Marisol. Daddy-O thought about that phat ass and pretty-ass face and reasoned he wouldn't want to be disturbed while he was up in that pussy either.

A knock on the door startled Daddy-O out of his daze. Stone, who had been lounging on the couch, was instantly on his feet and at the door. He turned from the peephole and mouthed to Daddy-O that it was E. Daddy-O dropped everything into one bag and slid it under the table before nodding to Stone to let E in.

"What's good?" E gave Stone a pound and stepped through the living room to where Daddy-O was. "Yo, where that nigga Prince?"

"He ain't here, son," Daddy-O said. "What's up?"

"You know Danny got knocked?"

That got Daddy-O's undivided attention. "Hell nah, when?"

"A few hours ago," E told him. "They said them boys jumped out and caught that nigga with a whole pharmacy. Yo, I ain't know Diego sold dope now."

"He don't," Daddy-O said and left it at that. "Shit." He slammed his fists on the table. "I gotta send somebody to see what's up with son."

"Man, with all the shit I heard he had on him, that boy is gonna have to sit up for a minute," E said. "Why the fuck would he be out with dope and crack on him?"

"Cause he's stupid," Daddy-O said seriously. He flipped his phone open to call Prince again and still got his voice-mail.

■

Cano's partner, who Prince had found out during the ride was named Juan, got out of the car first. He gave a brief look around to make sure no one was watching and opened the door for Prince. Prince sat there for a minute trying to think of a plan, but Juan snatched him roughly from the car. The cuffs bit into his skin, and he almost fell to the ground.

"I thought you people had good balance?" Juan joked, pushing Prince roughly toward the house.

The house was older than the rest on the renovated block, but not too old. The yellow paint was faded and chipping, but the house itself looked sturdy. Juan led Prince around to the side of the house while Cano led Marisol up the front steps. For a moment their eyes locked, and he almost felt pity for her, but he couldn't be weak. It was because of whatever she was tied up in that had him possibly walking to death's door.

Juan led Prince down a pair of rickety stairs into what appeared to be some sort of storm cellar. It reeked of urine and something else that Prince was all too familiar with, blood. The center of the basement was illuminated by a dull overhead light, casting the rest of the basement in shadow. Something gooey stuck to his bare foot, but he didn't look down to see what it was. When they descended into the foul-smelling basement, Prince heard a faint whimpering to his left. He squinted against the darkness and saw the form of a man. Much like him the man was naked, but he couldn't tell if he was handcuffed in the dim light. At Juan's prodding, Prince moved further into the musty basement.

"Have a seat." Juan slid a splintered chair over to Prince with his foot. "My boss will be with you in a second." With that, Juan went up the stairs on the opposite side of the room and into the main house.

"Fuck!" Prince yelled. His situation was getting uglier and uglier by the minute. He looked around frantically in the hopes of finding something to use for a weapon, but it was useless. He saw nothing in the empty basement that he would be able to use to his advantage.

"Yo," Prince whispered. The dude groaned, but didn't respond. "Yo, B, we gotta get outta here." There was still no response. Prince knelt down to see what was going on with the stranger and found that he wasn't even fit to walk, let alone make an escape. Someone had been beating the hell out of the dude for at least a few days, focusing mostly on his genitals. If that's what they thought they had in store for Prince, they might as well have shot him and got it over with.

As if on cue, Cano and Juan came down the stairs with some very nasty looking devices. Juan held a bucket of water that splashed over the lip of the bucket as he walked. Cano held two long wires with what looked like earmuffs on the ends. He stooped down in the corner and plugged the wires in, causing a faint humming to come from the cushioned ends. This was definitely about to get real ugly.

"I see you've met Felix," a deep, yet feminine voice from behind them. Prince looked past his abductors to see who the new voice was coming from. He could make out Marisol's form standing at the bottom up the stairs, but he was quite shocked to see who it was speaking to him.

She had to be in her mid-sixties to early-seventies. A floral duster hung about her like a tent as she moved closer to where Prince was standing. Her face was smooth yet warm as she smiled at Prince from behind tinted bifocals. A brass cane hung on one meaty arm, but it looked like it was more for show than actual use. On her thick hands she wore gardening gloves, that if Prince didn't know any better he would've sworn were splotched with blood. Prince looked from his surroundings to the grandmotherly old lady and felt like he was living in an episode of the *Twilight Zone*.

"They call me *Mommy*, and I hear you're called *Prince*?" She tried to be cordial, but Prince just stared. "You know, my sons rough you up a bit, but you don't have to be rude, negrito. If anything, I should be the one upset about my missing heroin."

"Ms., I'm gonna tell you like I told your sons; I don't know anything about any stolen heroin."

"So you tell me," she said, squinting at him through her tinted bifocals. "My daughter has been speaking much to me about you," she nodded toward Marisol, who was looking at the ground. "She tell me some things that maybe they true and maybe they not, no?"

"Ms . . ."

"Mommy," she corrected him.

"Mommy, I don't know what your daughter has told you, but I didn't steal any heroin. She gave it to me."

Mommy shrugged. "We find that out shortly."

When Juan and Cano started in Prince's direction, he automatically tensed. He expected them to try for him, but to his surprise they laughed and walked right passed him. The man who had been identified as Felix was grabbed and dragged roughly to the center of the basement. He pleaded and screamed, but the men ignored him as they looped the links to his handcuffs over a hook that Prince hadn't noticed hanging from the ceiling.

"Prince," Mommy drew his attention back to her. "The man you see is Marisol's ex-boyfriend, Felix. Much like yourself, he had a hand in the disappearance of Cano's heroin, but unlike you he's guilty of a far worse crime, plotting harm to my children."

"Please, Mommy," Felix whimpered. "I love Marisol."

"Oh, so you show your love by treating her like a whore?" Mommy's hand lashed out and slapped Felix across his face, sending blood flying across the room. Prince hadn't even seen her pull the straight razor that had just opened Felix's face.

"Now," she flashed her eyes on Prince. "My daughter has admitted to stealing the heroin, but Cano's money is still missing. What I want to know is what really happened? Now, if the story you tell me doesn't match what my daughter has said . . ." she nodded toward Cano.

Cano smiled and slipped on a pair of rubber dish gloves.

He picked up the cushioned wires and touched them together, producing a spark. Prince turned his head away, but Mommy's heavy voice called out to him.

"Don't you dare turn away, Mr. Heroin King of the Douglass Project." She grabbed Prince's jaw roughly in her hand. Her face was streaked with Felix's blood, making her look like a character in a Wes Craven movie. Mommy had a surprisingly strong grip for a woman, and had it not been for Juan keeping his gun trained on Prince he would've pulled away. "You watch what we do to men who betray *mi familia*."

Cano touched both of the cushions to Felix's chest, and the lights in the basement flickered. Felix jerked as hard as he could, but the handcuffs held. Felix howled like a wounded coyote as Cano pumped only God knew how much electricity through him. Only when the smell of burning flesh filled the basement did Cano stop.

Mommy turned her stormy eyes to Prince and hissed, "Now, how did you get your hands on my drugs?"

Prince looked from the gruesome scene around him and swallowed the lump in his throat. In the hood he was one of the hardest niggaz out, but in the face of Mommy and her crew, he decided to let honesty prevail where balls would do him no good. He went on to tell Mommy and Cano the tale of how he and Marisol had become involved, and she offered him the heroin to sell in the projects to break away from Diego. He also told them how Marisol had led him to believe that she and Cano were partners, therefore making him think the deal was legit. He wasn't sure if they bought into it or not, but the truth was all he had to bargain with.

"A very interesting story," Mommy said. "Cano?" she looked to her son.

Cano walked up to Prince. He was no longer holding the torturing devices, but Prince was still on guard. Cano looked into Prince's eye, and Prince held his stare. Even though he knew that Cano could and probably would end his life, he wouldn't cower.

"It sounds like something Marisol would cook up," Cano said. "You know, she's been putting her nose where it doesn't belong since we were kids."

"Cano, I just wanted to show you that I could help," Marisol said.

"Marisol, blowing over a hundred grand of our money is not helping. You give a thief and a novice almost a whole kilo of heroin and not collecting anything from it is not helping."

"What about the five grand?" Prince spoke up. There was no way he could prove that that was the money he had brought back to Marisol for the drugs, but he figured it couldn't hurt to mention it.

"What?" Cano and Mommy asked at the same time.

"The five grand that you found at Marisol's was the money I was bringing her back off the ounce she fronted me," Prince explained.

Cano stepped closer to Prince and looked him in the eyes.

"Negrito, you mean to say that you moved an ounce of heroin on a crack block in that little bit of time?"

Prince shrugged. "What can I say? I've been hustling since I was ten."

"Juan," Mommy spoke up. "Get him something to wear." Mommy turned back to Prince. "Now, Mr. Heroin King, tell me this story of how you did what Felix could not."

While Prince dressed in the sweat suit Juan had brought him, he told the story of how he had cut the heroin and broke it down into packs like they did the coke. He informed them of the heroin drought on the Westside and how the dope had moved easily. He was sure to leave out the part about how he needed Scatter and Ebony to cut it, feeling that he still needed some kind of leverage with Mommy. By the end of his tale, Mommy looked puzzled and Cano was just shaking his head.

"That is quite a story," Mommy said.

"It's the truth," Prince responded.

"I believe you. Cano," Mommy said something to Cano in Spanish. He protested, but she wasn't trying to hear it. Reluctantly Cano went off to the upper levels of the house to do whatever Mommy had told him. "Prince." She turned back to him. "I'm afraid we've been poor hosts to you. It was nothing personal, but I had to get to the bottom of what happened to my heroin."

"I'm good, I just wanna go home and forget this shit ever happened," Prince insisted. As he was speaking to Mommy,

Cano came back into the basement holding a folded newspaper. He glanced at Prince then placed the newspaper into his mother's outstretched hand.

"A gift," Mommy said, holding the newspaper out to Prince.

"What's in it?" Prince asked suspiciously, but still didn't reach for the roll.

"Double what Marisol gave you. Bring back the same fifty-five and everything else is yours. It's just my way of saying that I'm sorry for what my daughter did. When you're finished with that, come back to Cano and he'll start you on your first half-bird of H. Do you think you can handle it?"

The logical side of Prince's mind told him to tell her *hell no* and hightail it home, but the greedy-ass hustler that lurked within his heart said to jump on it. Things went sour with Marisol, but that didn't mean he wasn't supposed to make the most out of it.

"Yeah, I can handle it." Prince took the roll.

"Muy bien." She hugged him, oblivious to the blood she was getting on his worn grey T-shirt. "Prince, I sorry we had to meet like this, but I hope making you a rich young man will make up for it.

Prince looked from the rolled up newspaper in his hand to Mommy and said, "Enough money will make even the most lethal wounds seem superficial." Prince was heading for the door, but Mommy's voice stopped him.

"Don't hate my daughter, negrito. She is not from the streets, so she doesn't see the insult in what she did to you."

Prince looked at Marisol's saddened face. She still had a lot to answer for, but that would come later. For now he was just trying to get back to the block.

CHAPTER 15

Daddy-O immediately knew something wasn't right when he saw Prince. Physically he seemed fine, but he was dressed like an escaped mental patient. Prince whispered something to someone inside the truck and started making his way up the path. Diego was posted up by the center, watching Prince curiously. Prince either didn't see him or didn't acknowledge him, never breaking his stride.

"Yo, where the fuck you been?" Daddy-O asked.

"Come with me to change right quick," Prince said, continuing toward his building.

Along the walk, Daddy-O brought Prince up to speed on what he'd missed during the two days he was MIA. Hearing that little Danny got popped stung. He knew Danny wasn't built for the game, but he let him rock to keep him from becoming someone else's meat. It had almost served the little nigga right for going against what he was taught and walking

147

around that dirty. Greed had been the downfall of many a man, and Danny was further proof of that. But wrong or not, Prince had to get him out of jail.

Prince took a quick shower and threw on some sweats and a white T-shirt with his white-on-white Airs. From a lockbox that he kept under his bed, Prince produced a .40 cal. It wasn't as big as the nine he was used to working with, but it was easier to conceal under the sweats and had just as much stopping power.

"So, you plan on telling me why you came back to the hood looking like a nigga fresh off the boat?" Daddy-O asked.

"My nigga, I've had one hell of a day. Twist something up while I run it down to you," Prince said. While Daddy-O sat on the edge of his bed rolling a blunt, Prince told him about his kidnapping.

"Man, we need to rock that bitch and let her brother hold something too." Daddy-O lit the weed.

"Nah, we worked it out," Prince assured him.

"Fuck you mean y'all worked it out? Son, them niggaz had you tied in a basement ass naked. What the fuck could they possibly have offered you to make it right?"

"I can show you better than I can tell you, kid." Prince sat the newspaper on the bed and slowly unfolded it. In the center sat the two ounces, neatly wrapped in plastic wrap.

"Is that what I think it is?" Daddy-O smiled at the ounces.

"You know it," Prince beamed. "The old broad says that after we're done with this, we can get that real weight. We in business, baby!" Prince gave his man a dap. For the next hour the two men smoked blunts and discussed their plans for the future.

■

It was almost a week before the heat started to die down. The crack business was still flourishing, and Prince's dope operation was starting to gain momentum. They had little dudes roaming through the projects and the surrounding areas with packages of dope. He didn't want them sitting in one spot for too long, because Diego might catch on, so he kept them on the move. Either Scatter or Ebony would hit one of the young boys on their Boost phones, which Prince made sure everyone was equipped with. The two dope fiends had proven to be loyal and invaluable in getting Prince's thing going, and he made sure they wanted for nothing. Scatter and Ebony were holding good dope at all times.

Six days after Prince had gotten the dope from Cano, it was almost gone. Fiends were coming from Harlem and all points north to ride Prince's train. The dough was pouring in, and he couldn't wait to drop it off to Cano so he could get the half-bird Mommy had promised.

After putting Mommy's bread off to the side, Prince paid his workers. He then took fifteen hundred and put it to the side for Danny. He was still locked up, but that didn't mean he wasn't going to need a little something to help fight the case. The public defender was cool for the arraignment, but when Danny went to trial he was going to need a paid mouth-piece. He knew Danny was going through the motions sitting up on Riker's Island waiting for them to make bail, but there was a method to Prince's madness. It would look real suspect if they went in and got him out right away. Danny hadn't had a job in God knew how long, and his mother was on a fixed income so there was no way to account for the money that quick.

The next thing he did was drop a thousand dollars on Keisha and send her down to Tiffany's for him. She returned with a beautiful sterling set consisting of a necklace and bracelet. Though Marisol was still thoroughly etched onto his shit list, there was no sense in him not caking off her. As long as she was happy, Mommy and Cano would keep him correct with the dope. He dug Marisol, but he *loved* paper.

Prince packed Mommy's money in a manila envelope and stuffed it in his pants. With the Tiffany's bag dangling from his wrist, he headed out the door. As he was touching the avenue to get in his waiting cab, he bumped into Killa-E. The boy obviously had something on his mind because he was sporting a five o'clock shadow and an expression like he had lost his best friend.

"E, what it is?" Prince gave him a dap.

"Shit, out here stressing. I know you heard what happened?"

"Yeah, niggaz said you wigged out on ya baby mama's boyfriend? They said you popped the nigga and all that." Prince recalled hearing through the grapevine.

"Yeah, I blacked out on the nigga cause he was talking shit, but I didn't shoot him, I pistol-whipped his ass," E lied. "They're charging me with assault and possession of an illegal firearm. I got lawyer fees up the ass."

"That's a bad break, my nigga," Prince sympathized. "What kind of time you looking at?"

E thought about it for a minute. "On the assault, probably a two to six if this lawyer is any good. That Jew bastard is charging me fifteen thousand to do the case, so I'm out here day and night trying to get it up."

"True, so I know you working overtime at that spot downtown?" Prince said, with an idea forming in his head.

"I'm rocking these niggaz as best I can with what I go to work with. I ain't holding enough weight for it to be more than a side hustle and ain't nobody trying to front me nothing. Knox plugged me to these outta-town niggaz he fuck with from upstate though. They come through and spend a few Gs with a nigga from time to time on the white, but that ain't really their thing. They say that dope is the new drug of choice up in Binghamton. Just my fucking luck that all the dope connects I know out here got shit that can't hold more than a three . . . four if I get lucky. I'm telling you, P, if it wasn't for bad luck I wouldn't have none."

Prince silently measured E's words. E was in a tough situation, and Prince needed an alternative outlet for the blow he was moving. Not only had E unknowingly provided Prince with that much-needed outlet, but he had possibly found a way to help Prince triple his money. His mouth began to water at the thought of what he would charge the out-of-town cats for what he was holding on to.

"Yo, E, I'm about to put you on to something, but if I find out you told anybody not only am I cutting you off, but I'm fucking you up," Prince said seriously.

E's eyes flashed hurt. "Prince, we've known each other too long for you to even feel like you've got to come at me like that. What's popping?"

Prince sighed. "A'ight, check it out. I just came up on some shit that's got the whole Westside popping. . . ."

■

During the time he spent talking with E his cab had left him, forcing him to call another one. While he was posted up waiting, he heard a voice that sent chills up his spine.

"Prince, what's good?" Diego smiled at him.

"Ain't nothing, my dude," Prince gave him a dap. He made sure that his voice was neutral.

"I've been trying to get at you for the last few days but

keep getting the voicemail. You ain't fucking with me, poppy?"

"Oh, I lost my phone a few days ago, that's all." Prince played it down like it was nothing. His phone was actually still over at Marisol's. He made a note to himself to get it back when he got a chance.

"So what's up, you ready to get back on the money?"

"You know I'm always about my chips, baby, that ain't changed," Prince said eagerly. Though he was making respectable money slinging dope, the money he got with Diego was still his primary source of income.

"That's what I like to hear," Diego clasped him on the shoulder. "So, that means no more funny business, right?"

"No more what?"

Diego's face became serious as he spoke. "Prince, I haven't gotten to where I am in the game without watching everything that goes on around me. I know you've had your boys moving this new shit you got with mine."

"Diego I . . ."

"You don't have to explain, Prince. I blame this on myself." This statement threw Prince off. "See, people told me, but I didn't see the writing on the wall. You were born to lead, my man, not live in the shadow of someone else. I see that now. This is the reason why I'm gonna put you in charge of your shit. You win, poppy."

Prince looked at Diego disbelievingly. For as long as he had petitioned him for his own thing, Diego had fought him on it tooth and nail. Now he was supposed to believe that he had a change of heart overnight? There had to be more to the story.

"What's the catch?"

Diego looked at him as if he was genuinely hurt. "There's no catch, poppy. Of course you'll pay the street tax."

"Of course," Prince agreed.

"Then there's the little matter of the heroin."

"Oh, that's not a problem, D. I don't mind kicking in a tax on that as long as I can rock in the hood with it."

"Oh, no. I don't want a tax on the blow. I want in." Prince made to protest, but Diego waved him silent. "Prince, it's been a long time since there was good dope down this way, and I hear the shit you got is some of the best. Me being a natural business man, I'm trying to capitalize on it. From now on we put our money together on the dope and become partners, fifty-fifty, amigo."

Prince couldn't believe the nerve of Diego. A few days ago he suspended him from the block, now he wanted to be his partner. Prince wanted to tell him to go fuck himself, but he settled for, "D, I don't really need a partner on the dope. Me and my people got an understanding about this, so let's just keep it with the street tax. Look, I'll even bump it up to twenty percent as opposed to fifteen."

Diego looked at Prince as if he couldn't believe he was talking to him like that. "Who the fuck are you to give me a handout? Prince, *I* made *you*, not the other way around. Had you been anybody else hustling on my block, I would've had one of your own soldiers put something hot in you, but you're my little man so I let you rock. Don't you think that entitles me to a little something?"

Prince was so shocked by the move that he just stood there. Diego was still talking, running down the new arrangement between Prince and him. The arrogant bastard even had the nerve to suggest that Prince introduce him to the connect. After he was done, Diego patted Prince on the cheek and headed up the block. Prince watched him leave, feeling nothing but contempt for the man.

There it was. Diego had laid the gauntlet, and now it was Prince's turn to react. Diego had to be out of his fucking mind if he thought that Prince was just going to allow him to try and muscle his way into his heroin business. Prince would see him dead first. Wiping the spot on his check where Diego had touched him, Prince hopped in the cab to Queens.

CHAPTER 16

$\mathcal{J}$ail was turning out to be a less-than-pleasant experience for Danny. He had spent his first night at the police precinct where they grilled him for hours about his position in Prince and Diego's organization. Apparently the local police thought that Prince was one of Diego's partners as opposed to an employee. Danny kept his mouth shut, only speaking to say that he wanted to see a lawyer. Daddy-O and Prince had always taught him never to say anything to the police and let your lawyer do the talking. And he was determined to follow their lessons to a T during his stint.

The next morning, Danny was at 100 Centre Street to see the judge. Just after lunch that afternoon, he was called down to meet his lawyer for the first time. From the moment he met the public defender, he didn't like the man. He was a short white dude with thinning hair and a wrinkled suit. As soon as they sat down, the man started talking about a plea bargain.

Danny got uptight, stating that it was the lawyer's job to fight for his freedom, and this would've been true had it been a paid attorney as opposed to a public defender.

What most people learn their first time going through the system is that a public defender doesn't actually try to insure that you don't do time, they just try to make sure you get as little time as possible. Whether you go to jail or not, the city still pays their salary.

The public defender tried to explain to Danny that being on probation for the same thing that had knocked him wouldn't sit well with the judge. Two years prior, Danny was caught selling coke inside a nightclub. Because of his age he had escaped with five years felony probation. Now he found himself in yet another bad situation.

Of course Danny wasn't trying to hear about a plea bargain and belligerently said "Not guilty!" when questioned by the judge. The judge rambled off some things he didn't understand, gave him a date to come back, set his bail at twenty thousand, and called for his next case.

Danny was then moved to the *Tombs*, which was just two buildings down from the courthouse. The first thing Danny did was call Daddy-O and update him on the situation. Daddy-O told him to sit tight, and they would get him out in a minute. Thankfully the Tombs weren't as bad as he thought they would be. Of course they were crowded, filthy, and the COs treated you like shit, but Danny knew quite a few people so his stay wasn't that bad. Danny thought he would just kick back and enjoy the ride until Prince and Daddy-O got him out. No sooner than he got comfortable, they shipped his ass to Rikers Island.

Though it was supposed to be one of the largest facilities in the country, it still felt like they were packed in. Whereas everyone was grouped in together at the Tombs, Rikers Island was as segregated as the sixties. Bloods over here, that's a Crip house, this phone is for the Puerto Ricans. It was deplorable living conditions and heavy tension. He had been coming from the commissary the other day when he saw this kid run up the line with a razor and slit several bags, while his mans and them swept through and snatched the spoils. After a week in, Danny felt like he was ready to hang himself. It was a welcomed escape when he was informed that he had a lawyer visit.

Danny expected to be led to the area where he would normally meet his lawyer but wasn't. Instead the CO escorted him to a small room on the other side of the building. He ushered him inside and slammed the door behind. Danny recognized his weasel-faced lawyer, Coalfield, but the other man he didn't know. The man was immaculately dressed in a midnight blue suit and wire-rimmed glasses. He smiled broadly at Danny and motioned for him to sit down.

"Danny," Coalfield began, adjusting his brown tie. "This is assistant district attorney Michael Stern." Danny got ready to say something, but Coalfield held up his hand for silence. "Now, I know you've expressed that a plea bargain is out of the question, but I think you need to listen to what he has to say."

Danny glared at the lawyer viciously. He had already told Coalfield that he didn't want to cut any type of deal, but after the week he had endured within the halls of C74 he figured it couldn't hurt to listen. "Talk," he said to Stern bitterly.

"Daniel, I'm not gonna sit here and try to bullshit you because you're too smart for that, so I say let's cut to the chase," Stern told him as he flipped open a large folder. "You were picked up holding twenty bags of crack-rock and eight bags of heroin. Couple that with the fact that you're already on probation, and I'd say you're fucked pretty good."

Danny cut his eyes at Stern and chuckled. "Man, I ain't trying to hear nothing you gotta say. I don't do deals. I'll fight the case and if I lose, I'll do my time like a man. The hood will still be here when I touch down."

Stern and Coalfield exchanged comical glances. Stern closed the folder and placed his elbows on the table. "How fucking stupid can you be?" he asked bluntly. "Danny, do you think we don't know who's doing what in those projects? We know what you were selling and who you were selling for."

"Those was my drugs. I wasn't selling for nobody," Danny insisted.

"Give me a fucking break here, Danny. You can play that tough guy shit all you want, but you and I know what the real deal is. You're a third-rate nobody that'll probably end up sucking some buck nigger's dick if you get shipped up north, but fortunately you have that working in your favor. Danny, I don't wanna send you to jail. Hell, someone will probably murder you before long, saving me the paperwork it would take to prosecute you. But I do want your bosses. Give us something on Diego. Hell, we'll even take Prince at this point, but you gotta give us something to turn you lose."

"Man, if you called me in here to insult me, I'm going back," Danny stood up to leave but Stern's next words halted him.

"Eight-and-a-third to fifteen," He blurted out.

"What?" Danny stopped short.

"That's what you'll wind up with if you don't help us out. Not only are you a repeat offender, but you're a lieutenant in a continuing criminal enterprise. Do I have to spell it out for you?" Seeing the color drain from Danny's face brought a smile to Stern's lips. "Danny," Stern placed a recorder on the table and hit the button, "that's a long time for a handsome young guy like you to be behind the wall. Come on, Danny, help us to help you."

Eight-and-a-third years was a long time. Though Danny would still be relatively young at the end of his bid, the stretch definitely wouldn't be an easy one. He thought about the small roll he played in the organization and felt he didn't deserve it. Football numbers were reserved for bosses, and Danny was hardly a boss. They'd never get him to turn on

Prince, but maybe if he gave them Diego. . . . No, he immediately pushed the thought from his mind. He hated Diego just like the rest of them, but he would hate himself more for snitching.

"Nah," Danny said weakly. "I can't help you. Now, if you'd let me go back to my house . . ."

"I understand, Danny," Stern said easily. "Tough guy ain't gonna talk, huh? That's cool. Go ahead back to your dorm and pack your things."

"Pack my things? Where am I going?"

"Oh, we're transferring you to the Beacon," Stern said with a wicked smile. The Beacon was one of the most notorious buildings on the whole compound. Shit jumped off from time to time in all the buildings, but in the Beacon violence was the norm. If he thought he was having a hard time in C74, the Beacon would be like Hell.

"You can't do that. I'm supposed to be in the adolescent block!" Danny protested.

"Oh, we know that. But it seems that C74 is overcrowded, so we're transferring most of the tough asses to the Beacon. Maybe after spending a week in that place, you'll change your mind."

The CO came and escorted Danny back to his dorm for transfer. Along the way he allowed Danny to stop and cry in the hall, where the other inmates wouldn't see him.

■

"So, you spoke to that nigga, Prince?" Manny asked, taking deep pulls off a blunt of haze.

"Yeah, I spoke to him last week about that shit. I told that nigga I want half off that dope shit, nonnegotiable," Diego said.

"You think he's gonna go for it?"

"What choice does he have? Those are my fucking projects. If he don't pay he don't play, simple as that. Just to be on the safe side I'm gonna send him a little message." Manny didn't have to ask to know what Diego meant.

Manny nodded. "And what if he don't wanna go along with it?"

Diego looked at him seriously and said, "Then you do what you do."

CHAPTER 17

Prince had gathered his team for an impromptu meeting at the Wedge Hall in the Bronx, just off Hunts Point. It was a small strip club where you could go and watch the women shake their asses or even get yourself some pussy if your money and your game was right.

It was a special night as they were celebrating two things: Danny being home from Rikers and them stepping into the big time. As promised, Cano had given Prince a half-kilo of some of South America's finest. That's what he had been out of town putting together. The shit was even more potent than the Mexican blow he had gotten from Marisol and would draw in even more money because it could stand a heavier cut. This was the beginning of something big for the former small-time crack dealers.

"You really pulled it off," Daddy-O said, sipping a glass of Crown Royal.

"I told you I would," Prince grinned from behind his Corona. "From day one I told you niggaz that I was gonna get us where we needed to be, and we're finally here. No more small-time for us, my niggaz."

"Yo, we about to be some rich niggaz!" Jay said, nudging Danny. Danny just gave him a halfhearted smile.

Danny had been acting strange since he had come home from the Island, and it didn't go unnoticed by Prince. He reasoned that the young man must've been stressing about his upcoming trial. Prince told him not to worry, because they were going to get him the best lawyer possible. But in his heart he knew that Danny still might have to do some time. He had always warned his men about being careless, but Danny was hardheaded.

"Yo, kid, them niggaz in Binghamton went crazy over that new shit, Prince," E said from where he was seated. Prince had met heavy opposition when he broke it to his crew that he was putting E down, but he wasn't trying to hear it. Prince wasn't a greedy dude and believed that everyone deserved a chance to eat, even if E wasn't proven. Prince had a good heart like that. Daddy-O would always tell him that his good heart was going to get him into trouble, but Prince wasn't trying to hear it.

"As they should. We got the best dope in the city," Prince gave E a pound.

"Fuck the city; we got the best dope on the coast!" Daddy-O corrected him. Since they had started popping full-time, people were coming from as far as Yonkers to buy weight from them. They officially became the niggaz to see, and none of them were over twenty-three.

"Yo, I heard Diego ain't too happy about us going independent," Jay said. He looked like a little kid sitting there in an oversized football jersey and a fitted cap.

"If he's mad, he better scratch his ass and get glad. I made him an offer, but he wanted more, so fuck him," Prince said finally.

"Yeah, but a nigga is gonna miss that crack money, man. Not every fiend is a dope head in the projects," Stone pointed out.

Prince moved around the table and draped his arm over Stone's shoulder. "My dude, didn't I tell you I was gonna take care of you? I'm working on something with my connect to get us a brick of that white too."

"Damn, these niggaz got everything! When are we gonna get to meet him?" E asked.

"You ain't," Prince said flatly. "This is a business arrangement not a social group. I'll continue to deal with the connect directly."

"Yeah, but God forbid if something were to happen to you, we'd be cut off," E said.

"Don't trip off that, cause I don't plan on going nowhere. Even if I do get caught up, Daddy-O knows how to contact who needs to be contacted."

"I see," E said, clearly feeling slighted.

Daddy-O didn't make it obvious, but he was watching E. There was something about the kid that didn't sit right, but he couldn't put his finger on it. Daddy-O didn't give a fuck what Prince said, if E tried some funny shit he was going to lay him down.

"Yo, I wanna propose a toast," Sticks said. "To the team!"

"Word, B, to the team," Daddy-O echoed.

Prince stood and raised his glass. "Let no man here place himself above this union, lest they be consumed by this union." Everyone nodded in agreement and touched glasses.

■

The crew drank and partied well into the wee hours of the night. The strippers peeped their style and paid extra special attention to the balling young cats in the cut. Even little Danny had managed to come out of his funk long enough to get some head from a big-butt Spanish chick in the corner. It was all good until Prince's phone rang.

"Keish, what up?" he spoke into the phone.

"P, where you at?" she asked frantically.

"Me and my niggaz is in the BX, what's good?" He tried to stay calm but her tone was making him nervous.

"Yo, y'all need to get back here, now!"

"Keisha, tell me what's going down?"

"Man, the spot just got hit."

"Hit, damn! How did the police know where to rush?" he asked thinking about what he was going to tell Cano about the product they had lost. He didn't have all of the drugs in the spot, but most of them were up there. At least a quarter-kilo of blow and two hundred grams of coke they had left over from Diego's stash.

"Nah, these weren't the police. These was stickup kids." She went on to tell Prince how she had seen the boy Vince lingering around on their side of the projects. Being that she didn't know what had gone down with Jimmy, she didn't think anything of it. But when she saw him rush up in the building with two Spanish kids, she knew something was wrong.

"Fuck!" he yelled into the phone. "What about them niggaz I had out there?"

Keisha sucked her teeth. "Them bitch-ass niggaz ran when it popped off. The only one who tried to hold it down was little Gene."

"Where is he now?" Prince asked. Keisha was silent. "Keisha, where is Gene?"

"Prince, that nigga gone," she said, just above a whisper.

"Fuck you mean gone?"

"Gone, P," she let out the sob that she had been trying to hold back. "The little nigga's body is still in the lobby."

Hearing this, Prince's heart sunk. Gene was just a baby trying to make his way in the world. Prince thought he was doing something noble by giving him a job, but only ended up sending him to his death. Gene had come from a good home with a cool-ass mother whom Prince knew very well. How was he going to tell her that her little boy was gone?

"Prince, you still there?"

"Yeah, I'm here," Prince said in a choked-up voice.

"Yo, I'm gonna stay out here and see what I can find out, but y'all need to get back here ASAP."

"A'ight, we'll be there in a second. Thanks, Keish." Prince hung up.

"What's good?" Sticks asked, noticing the change in Prince's expression.

"We got hit, man." Prince recounted the story Keisha had told him to his crew.

"Yo, that's some bullshit!" Jay said. "That was my nigga, B. It ain't going down like that." Jay and Gene had been school chums, so his murder hit him the hardest.

"Oh, don't worry we ain't letting this shit ride." Stone patted Jay on the back. "Who did it, P?

"Keish said it was Vince from the other side."

"What? That pussy-ass nigga ain't poked his head out since we laid his homeboy down. He's a thieving-ass nigga, but he ain't no killer. Someone had to put the battery in him for him to jump out the window like that," Sticks said.

"She said he had two Spanish niggaz with him, but she didn't know their faces," Prince added.

"Let me take a stab in the dark on this one," Daddy-O put

his elbows on the table. "Right after you cut Diego out of the picture, Vince, backed by two unknown Spanish cats, runs up in the spot and robs us. It don't take a rocket scientist to see that Diego was behind this shit. But why kill Gene?"

"To send us a message," Prince said. "He knew Gene was our family, and he was showing us that he could hurt us. It's a lesson that I only need to learn once."

"What you wanna do, my nigga? I'm ready to ride on this nigga once and for all," Stone snarled.

"I'm with you on that shit. I still owe that faggot-ass nigga Manny for what he did at the liquor store," E said.

"You know if we go to war with Diego we gotta pull out all the stops," Sticks said.

Daddy-O looked at Prince. "I think this reckoning is long overdue. What you wanna do, P?"

Prince sat in silence for a moment. His eyes were glassy but no tears came. He had tried to offer Diego a compromise, and in return his one-time mentor had spit in his face. If Prince didn't do something, not only would he lose points in the hood, but Diego might come at another one of his people. It had to end.

"We gonna hand Diego his fucking head is what we're gonna do," Prince downed his shot of liquor. "Lets get this nigga for Gene."

■

E excused himself from the table while Prince and his crew plotted the demise of the former cocaine king of the Westside. Of all them, he probably hated Diego the most and would be glad to see him gone. After the hit was made, the police would be riding down on every known drug crew in a ten-block radius. E was going to make sure that when the shit hit the fan, his money wouldn't be fucked with.

He thumbed through his cell phone and scrolled through it until he found the number he was searching for. Using the banged up pay phone near the bathroom, he punched in the number. After the fifth ring a sleep-laden voice answered the phone.

"Lutz, this is E," E said into the phone. The music was so loud that he wasn't worried about anyone hearing him speaking to his lawyer. "Look, I know you're sleeping, but I need to see you like yesterday. Something big is about to go down in the projects."

CHAPTER 18

"**Y**o, I ran up in the spot and had them niggaz shitting in they pants," Vince bragged to the young wolves around him.

"Fuck outta here. Prince and them is the hardest niggaz out. You lying," one young man accused.

"Word to mine, kid. Yo, but them Spanish niggaz was extra with theirs. I felt kinda bad when son split shorty, shit," he said referring to Gene.

"Dawg, ain't you worried about that shit coming back to you?" another young man asked.

Vince looked at him as if he couldn't be serious. "Hardly, son. Diego got my back. He said when Prince is gone, I can take over the other side of the projects. I'm 'bout to be that nigga!"

"Yo, you better make me one of your lieutenants," the first young man said.

"Play ya cards right and I might let you rock," Vince teased. His bragging session was broken up by the sight of a sexy young lady approaching where they were standing. She was dressed in cut-off denim shorts and a tube top, with baby oil glistening over her body.

"What's up, Vince?" Keisha asked in her sexiest voice.

"Keish? Damn I almost ain't recognize you," Vince said, openly admiring her full breasts. "What's good?"

"You," Keisha said, licking her lips. "I'm trying to get high, where it's at?"

"I got some of that Cali back at the crib," he said.

"So what we still doing here?" she ran her hand down his chest.

"I'll see y'all niggaz in a minute," Vince said to the wolves.

"I see you, big dawg!" the first youngster said.

"Word, we can't come with you?" said the second young man.

"Nah, I'm gonna have to catch you on the come around," he said, watching Keisha's big ass as she walked ahead of him. He had been trying to fuck her for the longest, but she had never given him any rhythm. I guess the word was out that he was going to be the next man in the hood, and she was trying to get in on the ground floor. He rubbed his hands together and fantasized about what her lips would feel like wrapped around his dick.

■

Danny sat in the living room of his mother's house trying to suck the life out of the blunt he was smoking. There was so much going on that he felt like his head was spinning. He had spoken to the lawyer that Prince had secured for him, and the conversation wasn't quite what he wanted to hear. The lawyer advised him that he could probably get the charges lessened but doubted if he could make them disappear. Danny was definitely going to have to do some time, but how much depended on him.

He thought back to the meeting with Stern and the offer to set him free, and it seemed more tempting. He had been thinking long and hard about giving Diego up and saving his own ass. The DA said that all he would have to do is tell the grand jury how the man had distributed crack and cocaine throughout the projects. It seemed simple enough, but Prince's plan to murder Diego complicated that. If Diego died, then he would lose his bargaining chip and his ass was going to be shipped upstate to God only knew what kind of hell. He loved Prince and the crew like brothers, but the state was about to take a huge chunk out of his life, and he didn't know how comfortable he was with that.

Danny picked up his chrome .25 off the table and stared at it. He had contemplated killing himself, but didn't have the nerve to pull the trigger. That seemed to be the story of his life.

"I ain't no snitch!" Danny sobbed, while rocking back and forth with the gun.

Never in a million years would he have thought he would even be considering becoming an informant, but his back was against the wall. Though he loved Prince, it was absurd for him to think that his boss could beat Diego. Even if they did manage to kill him, his minions would surely hound Prince until he joined Diego. In his mind, sending Prince to jail would be like saving his life. At least that's what he told himself so he wouldn't feel like a total piece of shit. Either way Prince or Diego would have to be the sacrificial lamb. Danny pulled the business card that his lawyer had given him from his pocket and placed a call.

■

Vince lay back on his couch, moaning softly. Keisha was on her knees between his legs, giving him the best head he had ever had. She sucked him slow, then fast before relaxing her muscles and letting him fuck her throat.

Keisha took a breath and jacked his dick. "You like this shit, huh?"

"Oh, you know I do!" he almost shrieked as she went back to sucking him off. Vince felt himself about to cum when Keisha abruptly stopped. He opened his eyes to see what she was doing and his jaw dropped.

"What's popping?" Daddy-O stood over him, holding a sawed-off. Sticks was to his right holding a smaller gun in one hand and a hunting knife in the other. Both men wore wicked grins. Vince reached for the .22 that he kept stashed under the couch, but at some point Keisha had removed it and was now pointing it at him.

"What the fuck is going on?" Vince looked from Keisha to the two men.

"Retribution, my nigga," Sticks moved closer to him. "I'll bet you felt like a real man when y'all killed that little boy."

"What you talking about? I . . ." Daddy-O cut him off with a vicious slap to the face. Vince almost blacked out from the impact. He had heard stories about the brute force of Daddy-O's hands, but it was something else altogether to feel it firsthand.

"You picked the wrong mutha fuckas to rob." Daddy-O cocked the slide on the shotgun.

"Man, it was all Diego!" Vince tried to bargain.

"Oh, we know that. And we'll deal with that piece of shit soon enough." Daddy-O said, pressing the shotgun against Vince's face.

"Come on, man. Don't send me out like this." Vince was bawling like a child.

Daddy-O looked at him with compassionate eyes. "Nah," he lowered the shotgun. "I ain't gonna kill you, man."

"Thank you," Vince said, with tears in his eyes. "I promise, I'm gonna pack my shit and disappear. You won't ever see me again."

"I'm sure I won't." Daddy-O stepped back. "Sticks, rock this nigga!"

Vince's eyes go wide as Sticks advanced on him. He opened his mouth to scream but the sound was cut off when Sticks plunged the hunting knife into his gut. Wearing a smile like a kid on Christmas, Sticks pulled the knife across his gut and up to his neck. He wiped his hands on Vince's couch and stepped back. The last thing Vince saw before he left this world for the next was Keisha smiling as she placed her foot on the knife and forced it deeper.

■

A few blocks away, an equally gruesome scene was about to unfold.

Benny woke up feeling like he had gone five rounds with Mike Tyson. He had had the fortune of meeting a fine little freak the night before and they had fucked and snorted coke until sometime that afternoon. Shorty was still sleeping in the bedroom, but Benny's monkey had him up.

He was just about to sit down and get his sniff on when

there was a banging at the front door. He was about to ignore it, but the banging just got more urgent. "Hold the fuck on!" Benny shouted, pushing away from the table. He had made it halfway to the door when it shook violently, then flew open.

When Benny saw the battering ram he had assumed it was the police, but these were familiar faces spilling into the apartment. Stone led the charge, as Benny tried to run for one of the many guns that were spread throughout the apartment. He was grabbed by a pair of hands and thrown to the ground. Benny looked on helplessly as Prince came through the door looking like the devil himself.

The girl must've been awakened by all the commotion, because she came into the living room rubbing the sleep from her eyes. "Benny, what the hell are you . . ." the words died in her throat when she saw the living room full of armed men.

Naturally everyone expected her to scream, but to everyone's surprise she snuffed the closest man to her, which happened to be Stone, and bolted for the door. She had almost made a clean getaway when she ran smack into Jay, who was bringing up the rear. She tried to break fly and swing, which turned out to be a bad move. He blocked her punch and threw two of his own, landing them square on her chin. The girl's eyes rolled up in her head and she was out before she hit the ground.

"You niggaz got a lot of balls coming up in here!" Benny

said, struggling against the two soldiers who had him thoroughly pinned to the ground.

"Shut the fuck up." Prince stomped him in the midsection as he passed over him on his way to the living room. "Drag that mutha fucka out here!" he called over his shoulder, and the two soldiers did so with pleasure.

"You mutha fuckas are going down," Benny threatened as he was tossed roughly to the floor at Prince's feet.

Prince squatted down over Benny. "You know, you talk a lot of shit for a nigga that's on the ass-end of a pistol." Prince tapped his .40 cal against Benny's forehead for emphasis. "Now, take a wild guess why we're here?"

Benny looked from Prince to his team and back again. "Look man, I ain't got the key to the armory. Diego keeps it with him."

Prince snickered. "Baby boy, this ain't got nothing to do with guns."

"Then what do you want?" Benny asked, clearly terrified.

"To make a statement." Benny never saw the switchblade, but he felt it as Prince dragged it across his throat. Benny blinked as if he was trying to figure out what was going on. He let out a weak cough, squirting blood from the neat slash across his neck. Everyone watched in horror as Benny collapsed on his side and bled out.

"We out," Prince said, heading for the front door.

"What about the bitch?" Stone asked.

BLOW

Prince looked at the unconscious woman. "Leave her. When she wakes up she can tell Diego that we came by."

■

After Benny's hit, Prince had given his soldiers specific instructions to stay out of sight because of the heat that would surely be on all of them, but Jay couldn't. He had seen dead bodies before but never up close. Prince had sliced Benny's throat and left him to die like it was an everyday thing. Jay didn't know whether he was excited or repulsed by the act. He had tried to catch up on some much-needed sleep, but every time he closed his eyes he was haunted by visions of Benny's splayed throat.

Not being able to sleep, Jay decided to go cop some piff in the hopes that it would calm his nerves and help him to sleep. Prince had warned him that not only did they have to watch out for police but Diego's hit men. Not wanting to be the one who got caught slipping, Jay snatched up the .25 Prince had bought him on his way out the door. He had made it in and out of the weed spot without incident, but no sooner than he reached the corner did he see the flashing lights. Police seemed to be coming from everywhere at once, all rushing in Jay's direction. They tossed him roughly to the ground while he protested and screamed that he hadn't done anything, but they didn't buy into it. This wasn't some random bust; they had come for him specifically. When one of the

the pistol from Jay's pocket and smiled at him,
e was fucked in a major way.

■

m the moment he arrived at his office that morning,
ant district attorney Michael Stern knew it was going
: a hellish day. Over the course of the last week or so,
iglass projects had erupted into a civil war. From what he
d gathered from his sources, Prince and Diego had fallen
ut and were now standing on opposite sides of the fence.
The first stone was cast when a young boy named Gene was
gunned down during a botched robbery.

Word had it that Diego flipped out when he found out
about Benny's death. For two straight days Diego had sent
his soldiers through the projects opening fire on any and
everyone who was affiliated with Prince. They said he had
even kicked in the door of an old girlfriend of Prince's
and pistol-whipped her. Of course she wasn't talking. There
were several other reports of violence and still more pouring in.

The governor was on the mayor's ass, the mayor was on
the district attorney's ass, and Stern felt the wrath tripled. He
needed to get the situation under control in a major way and
the next two phone calls he received gave him a good starting point.

The first call was made by a confidential informant, via

his lawyer, confirming that Prince was behind several of the murders that had taken place. The kid was so deep up the ass with his own problems that he agreed to testify if it guaranteed him a pass. Two of Stern's most trusted men had gone to extract the CI and currently had him safely under wraps. Stern told the CI's lawyer that he could write his own ticket if the information he gave held up in court.

The second call was the icing on the cake though. Apparently a member of Diego/Prince's crew had gotten himself in over his head and was ready to play ball. Stern had done such a good job in rattling the young man that all thoughts of fighting the case had fled his mind. Little Danny had really thought he could get the long ride if he blew trial, which was bullshit. Stern knew Danny's new lawyer, and he was good at getting people off of charges that were supposed to stick. Danny might've had to do time, but it wouldn't have been as much as Stern had led him to believe. It was a good thing for the city that in this case, fear had won out over logic.

Between the two informants and all the paraphernalia they had found at the scene of the robbery, it would be enough to get warrants to search Prince and Diego's homes and maybe bring them in for questioning. Feeling pleased with himself, Stern decided to take the rest of the day off and get in some golfing while he waited for the warrants to be signed-off on.

CHAPTER 19

𝔄 week after Vince was killed, the projects were still on fire. The jump-out boys were taking no prisoners. Members of both Prince's and Diego's crews were being snatched left and right. They had even ran up in Daddy-O's house that morning, and he was now in custody at the Twenty-forth Precinct. Prince had Marisol call and make an inquiry about his status, but they refused to say what the charges were.

To make matters worse, word on the street was that the police were looking for him. Keisha had called him the night before and told him how homicide detectives were all over the projects showing pictures of him. They had even gone to his house, but of course he was already in the wind. What was fucking him up was how did they even know to look in his direction? Somebody was talking. He thought carefully on everyone who had a working knowledge of what they had going on and started using the process of elimination to narrow down his list of suspects.

Daddy-O and Prince were closer than real brothers so his loyalty was never even a question. Sticks and Stone were still young and liable to do some dumb shit, but snitching wasn't in their character. Next to Daddy-O they were the two most solid members of the organization. Danny wasn't a tough guy and seemed to be the most rattled about the situation, but Prince doubted if he was working for the other side. The charges the police had against him were bullshit and Prince had paid top-dollar to help the man fight the case. Besides that, Prince and Daddy-O had practically raised the young man. Even before he became a part of the team, Prince and Daddy-O had looked out for him, making sure he always had money for school and wasn't hurting for gear. This left Killa-E.

Daddy-O had brought it to Prince's attention that something wasn't right with E. Prince had defended E, telling Daddy-O that E was straight, but was he? E was seeing more money moving the heroin through the Binghamton cats than a lot of his soldiers in New York, so it didn't make sense for him to be the rat, but he did have open cases. No matter how cool E seemed, you could never tell what someone would do when their back was against the wall.

Just before the bullshit jumped off, E had pulled one of his disappearing acts. He had told Prince beforehand that he had to dip to Florida to check on a deal he was working out with a realtor on some property in Miami. It was no secret that he had long been trying to establish a legitimate business down that way. It just seemed funny that he had to rush off just before the police had started snatching his soldiers. It was after that that Diego's earlier warning had played back in his mind, and he wondered how trustworthy the kid really was?

After debating with himself about it, Prince called Cano. He had explained the situation to Cano about the raid and him suspecting that there was a leak in his crew. He'd expected some kind of seasoned wisdom from the older head but instead received a very stern warning. Cano told Prince that he had been making too much money for too many years to let a gang of black hooligans ruin it for him. Since Prince had brought his crew into the fold, it would be up to him to silence any voices that were speaking out against him. And on the issue of Diego, Cano simply said, "Every man bleeds, so every man can die. You need to decide who you fear more, him or me." That made it crystal clear to Prince that he had come too far to turn back. His enemies had to die or he would. He had done all he could to make the split amicable, but Diego wasn't budging. Picking up his cell phone, Prince decided that it was time to take the gloves off.

■

"See, this is why I fucking hate you. You're so bull-headed that you don't see the writing on the walls. It ain't the team, it's the coach," Sticks told Stone while stuffing a bottle of Bacardi light with a torn rag.

"And what the fuck do you know, you unathletic son of a bitch?" Stone shot back. "Isaiah Thomas is a proven champion and knows what it takes to win. It's your team that sucks."

"My dude, we've got like three all-stars and a two-time champion coming off the bench, but there's no direction. Trust me, once we get rid of Thomas, we'll start winning games."

"Whatever, son," Stone said, snatching up the two liquor bottles he had stuffed. "Let's do this and get it over with."

The two brothers hopped out of the unmarked four-door and gingerly strolled across the manicured lawn of the house. They stood in front of the two-story house and admired its vinyl sidings. To the passerby they seemed to be no more than two young men taking in the scenery until the first wisps of smoke rose. Stone heaved one of the bottles he was carrying and it crashed against the stucco roof, coating it in flames. One after the other the twins tossed the homemade cocktails, until the flames devouring the house could be seen for blocks.

Sticks moved as close to the house as he dared and lit his cigarette on the flames. "Now, that's a fire," he said, mimicking Eddie Murphy.

"You think Diego's gonna be pissed?" Stone asked, admiring their handiwork.

BLOW

Sticks slowly blew the smoke into the air. "Like I give a shit. Let's go home. The Pistons are playing the Suns."

"Another hopeless-ass cause." Stone patted his brother on the back as they headed back to the car.

■

"You think you're a real tough ass, don't you?" the red faced officer snarled at Daddy-O. "Well, being tough ain't gonna save you from spending the rest of your natural life in jail."

"Whatever, man," Daddy-O said as if he found the officer's very presence offensive, which he did. The day before Daddy-O had been at his crib getting the blow job of his life from the young girl with the lollipop he had met weeks prior on the bench. His pleasure ride was interrupted when his front door had come crashing in. Thinking it was a hit, Daddy-O grabbed his hammer and prepared to do battle. To his surprise it was the police.

He knew they were looking for drugs, which he didn't keep in his house, so they had nothing. They had him dead to rights on the gun possession, which he was sure he could get around. But surprisingly enough they didn't want him for either of the above. They were looking for a murderer. For the last four hours, they had been grilling him about the murders in the projects, but Daddy-O faked ignorance. They claimed that they had a witness who could place him and Prince at the scene of Benny's murder, which he knew was bullshit since he wasn't there. Whoever they had been speaking to obviously knew how inseparable he and Prince were, but they were wrong about that particular night.

He wasn't worried about them pinning Benny's murder on him because he could honestly say that he had nothing to do with it, but what bothered him was how they even suspected him or Prince for it in the first place. They were careful in their deeds, only letting their most trusted in on their plans. Someone had leaked. The first name to pop into Daddy-O's mind was E. The young man was as rotten as an overripe banana and as yellow as a fresh one in his book, but he was kept in the dark about what happened with Benny. Stone wasn't even a suspect because he had proven time and again that he would ride or die for the crew. Danny was a coward, but he had distanced himself when the gunplay came about. This left Jay.

The young boy was animated about extracting revenge for what Diego had done to his partner and was itching to air something out. Daddy-O had warned Prince against taking the young man along, but as usual Prince didn't listen. He reasoned that if Jay was gonna be a part of the team, he had to see what he was made of. Apparently he wasn't made of much or Daddy-O wouldn't be sitting in the interrogation room of the Twenty-forth Precinct.

"Take it easy on him, partner," the black detective said. "Mistreating the young man isn't gonna get us to the bottom of this any sooner. Sorry about that, kid," he said to Daddy-O, sincerely.

Since they brought him in he had been overly nice to Daddy-O. He had seen the good cop/bad cop routine enough times to know not to fall for it. When it came down to it, he was still the law, therefore the enemy.

"Okay, Dean." The black detective called Daddy-O by his first name to establish a sense of familiarity. "You and I know this is a bullshit charge you're in here on, so try to help us to help you. Somebody carved Benny up pretty bad, which we know isn't your style. Prince maybe, but not you. You'd rather beat someone up you had a problem with rather than kill them. Am I right so far?" Daddy-O just stared at the detective. "Anyway, I know that you had nothing to do with Benny's murder, but I figured you might be able to tell us who did. So what's up, you gonna tell us something?"

Daddy-O thought long and hard on it for a minute. In his most sincere voice he told the detective, "Yeah, man. I wanna tell you something. Go fuck your mother!"

Rage flashed in the black detective's eyes as he leapt across the table and grabbed Daddy-O by the front of his T-shirt. He tried to yank Daddy-O from the seat, but Daddy-O was too heavy. When he leaned over to get a better grip, Daddy-O threw all of his weight in the opposite direction, sending him spilling out of the chair and onto the floor bringing the black detective down with him. Daddy-O could've punished the detective if he wanted to, but instead he held him on the ground and laughed. His laughter was short-lived when the red-faced detective punched him in the back of the head, causing the room to spin. It took some effort, but the two detectives were able to hoist Daddy-O off the ground and sit him roughly back in the chair.

"You think that shit was cute, don't you?" the red-faced detective sneered. "Well, we can add assaulting a police officer to your list of charges." He was trying to intimidate Daddy-O, but the big man wasn't easily intimidated.

Daddy-O gave him a defiant stare. "Nigga, miss me with that bullshit. You think you dealing with somebody that's naïve to the law? If you had anything on me you'd have charged me with more than just gun possession. Now, take me back to my cell and give me the phone call you niggaz have been denying me since I got here. My lawyer is gonna have the both of you cocksuckers directing traffic outside the Holland Tunnel."

They had thought they could scare Daddy-O into talking like they had done the other ones, but he was made of sterner stuff. Daddy-O had been on the streets all of his life and respected the codes that governed them. Daddy-O was correct about them only having a gun charge, but what he didn't know was that members of their crew had already started dropping names to save their own assess. He was smiling now, but when they racked up enough to get him on conspiracy, he wouldn't be smiling anymore.

BLOW

■

Diego stood motionless, seething. At least two dozen people were standing around speculating on what they thought had transpired. The once-dry grass was now wet and muddy due to the excessive amounts of water the fire department used to douse the blaze. When he had first purchased the home, he couldn't have been more proud of himself. Coming from the slums of the Bronx all he had ever lived in were mice-infested tenements. He had vowed that if he ever blew up, he would cop a house for himself and his children. When the mantle of cocaine king came to him, he did just that.

It was a two-story house with a stucco roof and vinyl sides that he had had built to his specifications. He remembered how hard his son's mother had cried when he handed her the keys. Now, the only thing that was left of the two-year-old house was a smoldering frame.

"How could this have happened?" Carmen sobbed, kneeling in the muddy grass. She and Diego had been dating since high school, and when she gave birth to his son he wife'd her. Though she still had no ring to speak of, everyone knew she was his main lady.

"Carmen, get up," he took her by the arm and helped her to her feet. "The house can be replaced, mommy. The important thing is that neither you nor little Diego were inside when it went up."

"It's gone, Diego. Our beautiful house is gone," she said as if she didn't hear a word he said. "What are we going to do?"

"We rebuild. The house was insured, so we can use the money to either rebuild this house or find another."

"Afraid that might not be so simple," a voice called from behind them. A man dressed in a NYFD jacket carrying a clipboard came toward them.

"Excuse me?" Diego spun on the man.

"Mr. Suarez, I hate to be the bearer of bad news, but most policies don't cover arson."

"What do you mean arson? This was the result of faulty wiring or something, wasn't it?"

"Yeah, if the wires were made of glass," the inspector held up the remains of a scorched liquor bottle.

"You mean someone set our house on fire?" Carmen asked. "Why, how?"

"I wish I could say, ma'am. Do you or your husband have any enemies? Someone that might want to hurt you or get back at you for something? You know, I once met a guy who had a pissed off ex come back and torch his place, real nut job that chick was."

Diego glared at the man. "What're you, a funny man?" Diego grabbed him roughly by the collar of his jacket. "My house was just burned to the fucking ground and you're asking me, in front of my wife, if I had a mistress? What you should be doing is trying to find who did this to my place before I do!"

"Mr. Suarez, I'm just the fire inspector. The police will have to handle any other aspects of it."

"Then get me a fucking cop!" Diego shoved him roughly to the ground. The rattled fire inspector scurried away without bothering to try and wipe the mud off his khakis.

Diego paced through the wet grass, trying to gather his thoughts and plan his next course of action. As he paced, something caught his attention. It was so wet and horribly trampled by the parade of firemen on his front lawn that he almost didn't notice it. Kneeling, Diego picked up a cigarette butt from the grass and examined it. Whoever had done this smoked Newports, a brand of cigarettes that weren't common in the suburban neighborhood. Suddenly a light went off in his head. Though he might not have been the one to light the match, Diego knew Prince had a hand in what had happened.

"I'm gonna whack your ass once and for all," Diego growled.

"What are you talking about?" Carmen asked.

"Nothing, baby," he kissed her on the forehead. "Listen, take little D and go stay with your mother until we get this mess sorted out. I got some things I need to take care of," Diego started toward his car.

"Diego, our house is ruined and there's still paperwork to be filled out. Where are you going?" she called after him.

He turned to her and said, "To take care of something I should've dealt with a long time ago."

CHAPTER 20

"**D**amn, you the blackest ghost I ever seen!" Stone exclaimed, hugging Daddy-O when he walked through the door.

Daddy-O had been arraigned the day before and formally charged with possession of an illegal firearm. His bail had been set at $75,000 and to the displeasure of the two detectives, posted the next morning. It took the combined efforts between he and Prince to raise it, but he was back on the streets. He had just enough time to shower the jail-stink off of himself before he got the phone call telling him where the meeting would be held. Prince decided to keep it a secret up until the last minute to avoid any preplanned surprises.

"Fuck you, fat boy!" Daddy-O shot back. "Man, I ain't been home for a whole day and you starting right in."

"Welcome home, my nigga." Prince said with a weary smile. He and Daddy-O shared a pound/hug. It had been

197

several days since they had seen each other, and having his right arm back gave Prince a sense of comfort.

"You love throwing stones, don't you?" Daddy-O said seriously. Everyone knew that Prince was hot and the police were looking high and low for him. Though they were on the Amsterdam side in an apartment that, to their knowledge, the police knew nothing about, it was still not the smartest move for them to be out in the open like that.

"Can't nobody run me from my hood," Prince said in a tone that let Daddy-O, or anyone else who wanted to voice their opinion, that it wasn't up for discussion. "Come on in, we got business to attend to."

Once he had their attention, Prince addressed his team, "I assume it's no secret why I called you all here?" When no one answered he continued. "A few months ago we was all out here just trying to eat off Diego's plate, and now we're the ones doing the cooking and niggaz is hating. Diego trying to get at us and the police are on our dicks. But you know what, we knew it was gonna happen so we prepared for it. Let no one assembled here place himself above this union, lest he be consumed by this union, remember that?"

Everyone was silent.

"Well I remembered it," Prince continued. "It was an oath that we all took, but not everyone stuck to the script," his eyes swept the room. "Now, ya man Jay is gonna be the first of several casualties out this bitch by the time I'm done."

"Son, how we gonna get to the boy when he's in PC?" Sticks asked.

"Man, how many niggaz you know that's locked up?" Prince asked. "I got a young wolf on the job right now."

"Speaking of snitches, what's up with E?" Stone asked.

It was a question that Prince had hoped to avoid. E's sudden disappearance had everyone looking at him sideways. Prince wanted to believe that E's Florida story was the real deal, but it didn't sit right. To make matters worse, a young'n from the block had a court date at 100 Centre Street not too long ago. As he was riding the elevator, it happened to stop on the seventh floor and sure enough Killa-E was sitting there. For those not in the know, the seventh floor is where the DA's office was located, so it didn't take a rocket scientist to know what he was down there doing.

"Fuck him. Knox can move the rest of what he's got on the streets and then we're cutting them Binghamton niggaz off," Prince said. "I want everyone to get the word out that I got twenty grand on both them niggaz heads. Thirty if you finish 'em off before they can do any real damage. I want it to be known that in this camp, snitches will be put to death." His eyes seemed to linger on Danny a little longer than anyone else.

"What we gonna do about that nigga Diego? He acting like he want it, kid," Stone said.

"Man, I heard he's out there smoking any and everybody on this side. He ain't playing by the rules, Danny added.

Sticks shot him a disbelieving look. "Rules? My nigga, ain't no rules in combat. They hit us and we hit them, except we gotta make sure we hit them way harder than they hit us."

"Sticks is right. All this tit for tat shit ain't getting us nothing but hot," Daddy-O added.

"And that's why we're gonna finish this shit once and for all," Prince told his team. "Being that he and his bitch ain't got that big house to lay up in, there's only one logical place for him to move his family to. He's got a brownstone off 128th and Lenox."

"You mean to tell me that nigga was stupid enough to let you know where he rests his head?" Stone asked.

"He took me down there fronting like it was one of his lady's cribs that he kept work and guns in, but I peeped his government on some mail that was laying out on the counter."

Sticks rubbed his hands together greedily. "I can't wait to wax that skinny yellow nigga."

"Nah, that's my kill." Prince shook his head. "You and Stone are gonna handle Manny. I hear he's been a busy boy lately." Prince was referring to some information that he had gotten through the grapevine. It seemed that Manny wasn't so sure that his boy was gonna win the little tug-of-war with Prince and was trying to set up a connect with this young kid from out of Brooklyn who was looking to do his thing uptown. If Diego died, Manny planned to slide right into his spot.

"Prince, you're already hot as hell, man. You can't go and try to take out Diego on some Rambo shit. That's what you got killers for, son. Let us do our jobs," Sticks argued.

Prince placed a hand on Sticks's shoulder. "Young boy, you and your brother have always handled business for me on some grown man shit, and I love you for it, but this is something I gotta do. I want Diego to see my face when I relieve him of his brains."

"I'm coming with you too. If I let you go alone, you'd probably fuck it up." Daddy-O smiled.

Prince looked at his man. "Fo sho," he nodded. "Just make sure your ass don't get in my way," he teased him. "Danny," he turned to the youngster. "Your job is gonna be one of the most important."

"Me?" Danny almost jumped out of his skin. "Prince what do you need me to do?"

"The projects are too hot to sit on, so we gotta take this show on the road. I want you to round up what we got inside 845 and 875 and move that shit to 96th street. Guns, drugs, I want everything up outta there. Get Steve from down the steps to help you move the shit in his minivan. My man Chino is gonna hold it at his spot until we can establish another base. Danny, them people is about to shut the whole projects down, and I don't wanna lose one gram more than we already have, understand?"

"Sure thing, P," Danny said, thrilled that he wouldn't be asked to kill anyone.

■

Wayne was one of the young boys in the projects who was dying to get a rep. He had finally gotten his wish when a stray bullet from his gun hit a Chinese delivery man who was just trying to get home to his family. Wayne was currently in Rikers Island where he was awaiting trial on manslaughter charges. With his record he wouldn't be going home any time soon, so he decided to make the best out of a bad situation.

He was honored when Keisha had him and Prince on a three-way call. Since he was a shorty, Prince had been one of his ghetto heroes, and he was down to do anything for him. Though Prince never came out and said it directly, he knew what he was asking and was only too happy to handle it. It had been a snitch that pointed him out as the shooter so he did any and everything he could to make their lives hell. He had already stabbed two suspected snitches since he had been locked down, so one more was really no trouble. Besides, Prince was going to give him five thousand for the job, which went a long way in the joint.

Getting into protective custody was easier than Wayne had expected it to be. During lunch he had gotten into a fight with another inmate, leading to him getting cut. It was a minor cut, but Wayne told the guards that he was in fear for his life. They promptly moved him to protective custody, two bunks down from Jay.

Just after count, Wayne had struck up a conversation with

Jay. They had never hung out but knew each other by face from the projects. Wayne confided in Jay that he was an informant against Diego, which was a lie, while Jay confessed to being an informant against Prince, which was the truth. Before you knew it, they were swapping stories like two old buddies. It was all good until Wayne pulled out a length of coil from the bedspring that he had sharpened to a fine point.

Jay never even saw the first blow coming. When the coil tore into his kidney, it sounded like biting into a ripe plum. Jay tried to cover the wound with his hand, leaving his throat exposed. Wayne tore Jay up from gut to face and back again. By the time the COs pulled Wayne off the boy, there was barely enough of Jay's face left to identify him. The COs beat Wayne damn near within an inch of his life, but in the end it was worth it, because Jay's punk ass would never see the inside of that courtroom.

CHAPTER 21

The first thing that alerted Manny that something was wrong was the change in Greg's facial expression. He had gone from laughing to casting a shocked glare over Manny's shoulder. He had hit the ground just before bullets tore through the corner store window and Greg's chest.

Manny stayed crouched on the ground, scanning to see where the danger was coming from. Twenty yards south, he spotted two men on a motorcycle. Stone was yanking on the handle bars of the Yamaha, trying to bring it around into oncoming traffic. Sticks's emaciated form was perched on the back of the bike cradling a Mac-11. Manny had a serious problem.

The time for logical thought had passed as Manny's survival instincts kicked in. At the exact moment Sticks's finger depressed the trigger, Manny was in motion. Glass shattered and people screamed as bullets tore through Columbus. Manny darted across the bike's path, firing his 9 mm. He had hoped to hit Sticks or Stone, but only succeeded in ruining the light on the front of the Yamaha. The upside was that Stone lost control of the bike, spilling himself and his brother onto the street. By the time either of them had managed to get to their feet, Manny was bolting west on 104th street.

"Damn it, you're letting him get away!" Stone shouted as he tried to crawl from under the bike.

"You're the dumb shit that lost control of the bike," Sticks shot back. "Next time, I steer and you shoot."

"Man, stop running your mouth and go get that nigga!"

Sticks was reluctant to leave his brother, but Manny's death was their number one priority. Swapping the Mac for his brother's Desert Eagle, Sticks took off after Manny.

■

Steve sat in his car, which was idling in the parking lot on the Columbus side of the projects. Prince had called him earlier and said that Danny would be contacting him about moving their stash, but he had been waiting for almost a half-hour and there was still no word from him. He figured he would give Danny another ten minutes before calling Prince to tell him about the no-show.

Steve was about to light a blunt when he noticed flashing lights in his rearview. He tossed the blunt out the window thinking that the police were about to swoop in on the parking lot, but to his surprise they rolled right passed him. He turned around in his seat to get a better view and his jaw dropped. At least five police vehicles were speeding through the narrow walkway between 865 and 845. He wondered where the hell they were going, but he would find out before it was all said and done.

■

A bullet shattered a car window mere feet away from Manny, spraying him with glass. His chest burned, and he felt like he would collapse from exhaustion at any moment, but the sight of Sticks closing the distance drove him.

Sticks popped two quick shots, both missing Manny. He cursed and ran faster, hoping to catch up to Manny before he crossed the street. Stopping briefly he drew a bead square at Manny's back. Just before he pulled the trigger, the dirty son of a bitch wove between a group of women pushing strollers.

"Cocksucker!" Sticks shouted as he continued the chase.

When Manny crossed Amsterdam Avenue, he poured on the speed and was crossing Broadway in no time. His logic was that if he could make it to Riverside Park, he just might live through it. There was always heavy police presence in New York City parks, and this was one time he welcomed seeing the boys in blue.

Manny had made it to the park entrance when pain ripped

through his calf. He tried to keep moving but the bullet had shredded a muscle and his leg could no longer support his weight. In a last attempt at saving his worthless life, he tried to roll over and draw his gun only to have it kicked away. As he looked up into Sticks's midnight eyes, a warm trickle of piss ran down his leg.

■

With an audible grunt, Stone shoved the bike and was finally able to free himself. For the most part he was unharmed, but when he tried to stand it felt like his leg wouldn't support his weight. There was no way he could catch up to Sticks and Manny, so his best bet was to make an exit and hope his brother could finish the job on his own. No sooner than Stone turned to make his exit he found himself staring down the barrels of half a dozen guns.

"Drop the gun or I drop you!" the first officer barked. He had a nervous look in his eye and couldn't seem to quite keep his gun steady.

Stone weighed his options and figured he'd have a better chance beating it in court than holding court. "A'ight," Stone said, slowly lowering the gun. "Be easy."

No sooner than the gun touched the ground, the police officers were on him. They beat him with nightsticks, pistols, fists, and feet until Stone could barely move. As unconsciousness took him, he wished that he could see the look on Manny's face when Sticks killed him.

■

"Pop that shit now," Sticks taunted Manny, aiming the gun at his chest.

"Fuck you!" Manny shrieked, still trying to crawl into the park.

"That leg looks pretty bad," Sticks said, stomping on Manny's wounded calf. Manny let out a yell that sounded like a tortured cat.

"You pieces of shit, Diego's gonna kill you!" Manny threatened.

Sticks laughed wickedly. "I doubt that, since Prince is in the process of putting that nigga in a bag. Don't trip though, with all the money we're gonna make in the hood, we'll make sure your mama has the prettiest black dress you ever did see." Sticks was about to finish Manny when two police cars screeched to a halt a few yards behind him.

"Looks like you'll have to wait on that black dress," Manny burst out laughing at his narrow escape from death.

Sticks looked from Manny to the police who were filing out of their cars. After all they had gone through and overcome, it couldn't end like this. Manny would go to jail as surely as he would, but the judicial system couldn't punish people like Manny. He was a child of the streets, and only she could call him home.

"Fuck it!" In a blur, Sticks popped two shots into Manny's grinning face and bounded over the wall into the park. The police opened fire, but Sticks was already halfway across the open field. A bullet hit him in the shoulder, knocking him off balance and sending him crashing to the floor, and his gun flying into the brush. Pain shot through Sticks's shoulder, but his legs worked just fine as he trotted through the park, in the direction of the highway.

The blood loss caused Sticks to see spots, but determination wouldn't let him pass out. He had long ago vowed that he would rather die than spend the rest of his life in someone's prison, and Sticks considered himself a man of his word. Cars blared their horns and swerved as he hobbled across the highway. As he neared the edge of the water the horrible realization set in that he was trapped.

"Go ahead, I want you to run!" An officer sporting a buzz cut yelled, advancing on Sticks with his gun drawn.

"Take it easy, man. I ain't running," Sticks huffed. He raised his good arm and kept the injured one at his side. The officer with the buzz cut moved in on Sticks with a murderous look in his eyes. Sticks held no illusions about what waited for him. When officer buzz cut reached for him, Sticks swung as hard as he could with his injured arm, slicing the officer's throat with the box cutter he was concealing.

BLOW

Riverside Park was lit up like the Fourth of July as the officers all opened fire at the same time. Sticks got hit at least five times before he went sailing over the guardrail and into the Hudson River. His chapter in the game had come to a close.

CHAPTER 22

The block was quiet, too quiet in fact. Since 128th Street had been transformed from junkie heaven to up-and-coming Harlem real estate, the traffic had slacked up. You could still find an occasional cluster of people posted up, especially in the summer. But this night the block was still. There was movement in the shadows . . . scratch that . . . the shadows themselves seemed to move with the blowing wind. A man-sized figure peeled itself from the darkness and crept down the block in a crouch.

Prince made sure no one was watching him before closing the distance to Diego's brownstone. For the most part, all of the brownstones on the block looked roughly the same, but Prince retraced the route to Diego's brownstone with little effort. Maybe it was the barred windows, or it could've been the guard laying low in an unmarked car directly in front, but Prince knew he was in the right spot.

Had it been Manny, there was no way Prince would've been able to creep on him like that, but thankfully this guard wasn't quite as experienced. Faking drunk, Prince staggered the rest of the way down the block. When he got to the rear of the car he pulled out his dick like he was about to take a leak, and just as he expected, the guard got out of the car to bark on him about pissing. As soon as he opened his mouth Prince pointed his .44 Bulldog and pulled the trigger.

■

Diego sat in his leather armchair flipping through the channels on his big screen television. The house seemed empty with the absence of Carmen and little Diego. The fire was proof enough for her that the war between Diego and Prince was hitting too close to home, and she wasn't trying to get caught up in it. Taking little Diego, she went to stay with her mother until her husband got his business in order.

"Fuck her, I don't need nobody," Diego said to no one in particular. He tried to bring his drink to his lips to sip it, but only ended up splashing cognac on his tank top. He had been drinking all day long in the heat and found himself thoroughly fucked up. Manny had brought him home that afternoon and tried to stay with him, but Diego didn't want the company. He was going through the motions and wanted to be by himself, as he got sometimes. Only after promising that he would stay in for the rest of the night did Manny leave him.

Had it not been for Diego's bladder he probably would've sat in the recliner for the rest of the night, but nature called. He struggled to his feet and the room immediately began to swim. He staggered, knocking over the coffee table, bringing one of his security men rushing into the room.

"You okay?" the dark skinned man said. He had a scar that ran from his left ear to the bottom of his chin. Scar, as he was called, had only recently joined Diego's crew as an enforcer. He was from Brooklyn and had a reputation for brutality, which made him qualified to stand watch over Diego.

"Scar, why you come up in here like the damn police?" Diego slurred.

"I heard a noise and I came to check on you."

"Nigga, I'm good. Can't a grown man take a piss without tripping over one of you mutha fuckas?"

Scar shrugged. "My fault, Diego."

"Damn right it is!" Diego yelled as the door closed. Sucking his teeth, Diego stumbled drunkenly into the bathroom. He had barely freed his dick from his pants when the piss came raining out. Some of it splashed on the toilet seat and floor, but being that Carmen wasn't there, who was going to complain? He closed his eyes and leaned his head against the cool bathroom wall. Before he could finish his leak, a thumping noise coming from above him caused his head to snap up.

∎

Daddy-O cursed himself for being such a lummox. He and Prince had explored the possibility of there being guards in front of and inside of the brownstone, but the roof was something they hadn't encountered.

Daddy-O had broken into a brownstone that was still under construction two doors down from Diego's. He then made his way to the roof and began cutting across to Diego's building. He had just made it to the rooftop and was heading for the access door when a man stepped out from around the corner. He had his head bowed trying to light his cigarette, giving Daddy-O a split second to react.

When the man lifted his head, Daddy-O came across the bridge of his nose with the butt of the shotgun he was carrying. Blood squirted all over both of them, but it didn't seem to stop the man from drawing his weapon. He brought his pistol up and squeezed off a wild shot. The bullets chirped from the silent gun and bounced off the ledge at Daddy-O's rear. Daddy-O swung the shotgun like a club and knocked the gun from the man's hand. Moving with incredible speed, Daddy-O slipped behind the man and locked the shotgun around his throat. With a jerk he snapped the man's neck and let him fall to the floor. After checking to make sure there were no more guards on the roof, Daddy-O made his way to the lower levels of the brownstone.

■

Prince was sure that they had heard the gunshots inside the brownstone, and honestly he didn't care. The game of cat and mouse between he and Diego had gone on too long and he was determined to finish it that night. Placing himself to the side of the stairs, he waited.

A short Hispanic man came rushing out the front door to investigate what had happened. He looked around wild-eyed in every direction, except where Prince was hiding. Aiming his gun up, Prince popped the Hispanic man once in the throat and once in the gut. As he passed him on the way up, he put one more in his melon, putting him out of his misery.

Another man came rushing down the stairs waving a small submachine gun. Unlike the first man, he was much more cautious. Prince leapt from behind the door where he was hiding and tried to wrestle the gun from the man. Prince was strong, but this man was a brute. Instead of trying to pull against Prince, he pushed forward and slammed him into the wall. Before Prince could right himself the man hit him with a crushing right cross to the jaw. Prince came back with a hook of his own but only succeeded in enraging the man. He kneed Prince in the gut, doubling him over and followed with a hook to the back of the head. Prince was trying to struggle to his feet when the man put him in the sleeper hold. As the lights began to dim in Prince's eyes, all he could think about was how he had failed his team.

It was all but over for Prince, when there was a thunderous roar from behind them. Something slammed into the man's back, sending them both flying down the stairs. Prince had the wind knocked out of him, making it hard to focus. But when his vision cleared he saw Daddy-O's smiling face at the top of the stairs, holding a smoking shotgun.

■

"What the fuck was that?" Diego asked, stumbling out of the bathroom.

"We've got company," Scar said, checking the clip on his Beretta. "Get in the bedroom. I'll check with the others." Scar dipped off, leaving Diego alone.

Diego paced the room, trying to figure out what the hell was going on. Since he and Prince had started their little war, he had gained a new understanding of the young man. Prince was a man who was born to lead and Diego had stifled that. Instead of doing the smart thing and bringing Prince closer, he had pushed him away, making a very cagey enemy in the process. Now, his foolishness had followed him to his own doorstep. One thing was for certain, Diego wasn't going to go down without a fight.

Scar crept to the door, holding his gun at his side. Sweat

trickled down from his head and threatened to run into his eye, but he didn't dare release the grip on his gun to wipe it away. He had just placed his hand on the doorknob, when the whole thing came crashing in.

■

"Nigga, you could've killed me," Prince said in a horse voice.

"Shit, looked like he was gonna kill you," Daddy-O nodded at the dead man. "You ready to boogie?" He loaded another shell into the chamber of the shotgun.

"Ain't like we can turn back now." Prince checked his clip. "Let no man here place themselves above this union . . ."

". . . Lest they be consumed by this union." Daddy-O finished before he kicked Diego's door off the hinges.

The man who had been standing behind the door was caught completely off guard. The thick wood slapped him in the face, sending him backpedaling. Scar tried to bring his gun up but was hit with a blast from Daddy-O's shotgun. The impact sent him skidding up the hall and crashing into a door.

"Diego!" Prince shouted. "Let's finish this!"

In response to his request, the bedroom door flew open and Diego came out holding a gun that looked straight out of the Vietnam War. With a hellish grin, he squeezed the trigger. Prince managed to find cover behind a couch, but Daddy-O wasn't so fortunate. A bullet the size of a Chico Stick whistled through the air and tore into Daddy-O's arm. The force of the shot was so great that Daddy-O's arm was severed just above the elbow. The sight of his best friend's motionless body made Prince snap.

Disregarding his own safety, he popped up from behind the chair firing. Diego tried to swing the gun around to fire on Prince, but it was too awkward. The bullets tore bowling-ball-size holes in the wall but missed Prince. Diving across the living room, Prince just started shooting. A bullet slammed into Diego's chest sending the rifle flying across the room.

Momentarily forgetting Diego, Prince crawled over to Daddy-O's body. Cradling Daddy-O's head in his lap, Prince looked into the man's glassy eyes. At first he thought the man was dead, but seeing his chest rise and fall gave him hope. "I'm gonna finish it," he whispered to his friend before turning his attention back to Diego.

There was a smear of blood on the floor from where Diego had been trying to drag himself into the bedroom. His tank top was soaked with blood and he was breathing erratically, but that hadn't stolen any of the fight out of him.

"So, this is the part of the story when the student rises up against the teacher?" Diego coughed blood as he tried to laugh at his own joke.

"Nah, this is the end of the story, Diego. I loved you

like an uncle and you broke my heart," Prince said emotionally.

"Sometimes heartbreak helps to build character, poppy." Diego said, still trying to drag himself into the bedroom.

As Prince moved closer, he could see that Diego wasn't trying to escape into the bedroom, but trying to reach a gun that lay mere feet away from him on the ruined carpet. "You sneaky mutha fucka," Prince said, shooting Diego in his hand. Blood and pieces of Diego's fingers stained the carpet. "It's over, poppy." Prince raised the gun to Diego's face.

"Don't do it, Prince," a voice called from behind him.

Prince spun around and saw Scar limping toward him. Through his ruined shirt, he could see the bulletproof vest that had stopped the slugs from killing him. More to his surprise, a gold shield hung from around his neck.

"If you shoot me, you'll be killing a DEA agent," Scar explained. "Put down the gun, man. It's over."

Prince looked from Scar to Diego and thought about it. He wanted Diego dead, but not enough to give his own life in the process. No, it was better that he lived to fight another day.

IT'S A WRAP

THE NOTORIOUS DOUGLASS BOYS BROUGHT DOWN is what the headline of *The Daily News* had read. In the article it went on to detail the rise and fall of Prince Jones and his gang of vicious thugs. All through the trial, the papers ran articles on Prince and his crew, stating that they operated a continuing criminal enterprise that grossed nearly one million dollars a month, which was total bullshit. True, the dope money was sweet, but everything fell apart before they really got to enjoy it.

Prince tried to think positive about what the outcome of the trail might be, but in his heart he knew it was a wrap. In the end they had all pointed the finger at him. Killa-E had never really been down in Florida looking at real estate. As it turned out, he had traded Prince in to get a lesser sentence on the attempted murder. The funny thing is that more than half of the shit E said on the stand was a lie, but it didn't matter in the eyes of the law, as long as they got someone to prosecute for the crimes. Daddy-O had warned him time and again about E, but Prince wouldn't listen. Now he wished he had.

The cats from Binghamton didn't really exist. It was all a ruse to get Prince to send drugs over the county lines so they could make sure the charges stick. Knox had been a CI all along. For the past three years he had been setting dealers up all around the city in exchange for his freedom and all the coke he could snort. Of course there was no mention of the cocaine in court, but Prince wasn't stupid. Knox loved his habit almost as much as he loved his own life, which wouldn't be worth shit if Prince had it his way.

Even Diego lent his voice during the trial. It was laughable to see him on the witness stand trying to pass himself off as a poor immigrant whom Prince and his crew supplied drugs to. That mutha fucka even had the nerve to lie and say Prince had threatened his wife and young son at gunpoint. For all the bullshit he talked about what it took to be a real street nigga, he didn't know a damn thing about it. The former cocaine king of the Westside would be forever remembered as a stinking-ass rat.

One by one Prince watched them give their accounts and didn't blink, but when Danny took the stand his heart crumbled into a million pieces. Here was a young man whom he and Daddy-O had raised as their own telling the jury how he was the product of a broken home and Prince and Daddy-O had forced him into a life of crime. He even broke down and cried a time or two.

The real kicker was what happened to the drugs and guns he was supposed to be moving out of the spot. Danny never made it to meet Steve because while Steve waited on him in the parking lot, Danny was telling the police where they could find the stash. He was only facing a three to six, with the possibility of coming home in two-and-a-half, but he figured that getting out of doing a few short years in jail was worth a lifetime of friendship.

It took the jury two hours to find them guilty on all counts. When the verdict came down, the whole court room erupted. Marisol sobbed on her mother's lap while some of the young dudes from the hood cursed and caused a scene. Stone was so distraught that he tried to hurl his chair at the judge. All that got him was an ass whipping by the court officers and the promise of more time, as if they would be on the streets before they were old and gray anyhow. Prince just sighed.

The sentencing would come later, but there was no doubt in Prince's mind that the hag on the bench would look to throw the book at them. The only upside was that the state didn't push for the death penalty. With all the bodies connected to the crew, the DA surely could've pushed for the needle and possibly gotten it. Instead they would most likely have to spend the rest of their lives in prison. Being alive was a blessing that Prince should've been thankful for, but what good is a life in captivity?

■

    I say all that to say this: the game has changed. Back when men were men, there were rules and codes of conduct to make sure everyone got a piece of the American dream. Now, the game is full of rats and video gangsters. Young cats today are quick to get a pack and take it to the block, but always remember that karma is a bitch. For every action there is an equal and opposite reaction. When the lady of justice calls your number, what are you gonna do? Will you hold that football number like a man, or point the finger at the next nigga?

TURN THE PAGE FOR EXCERPTS
OF MORE G-UNIT BOOKS

from 50 Cent

DERELICT

By 50 Cent
and Relentless Aaron

DERELICT: Shamefully negligent in not having done what one should have done.

Prison: One of the few places on earth where sharks sleep, and where *"You reap what you sow."*

he note that Prisoner Jamel Ross attached, with his so called "urgent request," to see the prison psychotherapist was supposed to appear desperate: *"I need to address some serious issues because all I can think about is killing two people when I leave here. Can you help me!"* And that's all he wrote. But even more than the anger, revenge, and redemption Jamel was ready to bring back to the streets, he also had the prison's psych as a target; a target of his lust. And that was a more pressing issue at the moment.

"As far back as I can remember life has been about growing pains," he told her. "I've been through the phases of a liar in my adolescence, a hustler and thug in my teens, and an all-out con man in my twenties. Maybe it was just my instincts to acquire what I considered resources—by whatever means necessary, but it's a shame that once you get away with all of those behaviors, you become good at it, like some twisted type of talent or profession. Eventually even lies feel like the truth . . .

". . . I had a good thing going with *Superstar*. The magazine. The cable television show. Meeting and comingling with the big name celebrities and all. I was positioned to have the biggest multimedia company in New York; the biggest to focus on black entertainment exclusively. BET was based in Washington at the time, so I had virtually no competition. Jamel Ross, the big fish in a little pond . . .

"And of course I got away with murder, figuratively, when Angel—yes, the singer with the TV show and all her millions of fans—didn't go along with the authorities, including her mother, who wanted to hit me with child molestation, kidnapping, and other charges. I was probably dead wrong for laying with that girl before she turned eighteen. But Angel was a very grown-up seventeen-year-old. Besides, when I hit it she was only a few months shy from legal. So, gimme a break.

"In a strange way, fate came back to get my ass for all of my misdeeds. All of my pimp-mania. That cable company up in Connecticut (with more than four hundred stations and fifty-five million subscribers across the country) was purchased by an even larger entity. It turned my life around when that happened; made my brand-new, million-dollar contract null and void. There was no way that I could sue anyone because lawyers' fees are incredible and my company overextended itself with the big celebrations, the lavish spending, and the increased staff; my living expenses, including the midtown penthouse, and the car notes, and maintenance for Deadra and JoJo—my two lovers, at the time—were in excess of eleven thousand a month. Add that to the overhead at *Superstar* and, without a steady stream of cash flowing, I had an ever-growing monster on my hands.

"One other thing, both Deadra and JoJo became pregnant, so now I would soon have four who depended on me as the sole provider. Funny, all of this wasn't an issue when things were lean. When the sex was good and everyone was kissing my ass. Now, I'm the bad guy because the company's about to go belly-up."

With a little more than two years left to his eighty-four-month stretch, Jamel Ross finally got his wish, to sit and spill his guts to Dr. Kay Edmonson, the psychotherapist at Fort Dix—the Federal Correctional Institution that was a fenced-in forty-acre plot on the much bigger Fort Dix Army Base. Fort Dix was where Army reservists went to train, and simultaneously where felons did hard time for crimes gone wrong. With so many unused acres belonging to the government during peacetime, someone imagined that perhaps a military academy or some other type of income-producing entity would work on Fort Dix as well. So they put a prison there.

The way that Fort Dix was set up was very play it by ear. It was a growing project where new rules were implemented along the way. Sure, there was a Bureau of Prisons guidebook with regulations for both staff and convicts to follow. However, that BOP guidebook was very boilerplate, and it left the prison administrators in a position in which they had to learn to cope and control some three thousand offenders inside of the fences of what was the largest Federal population in the system. It was amazing how it all stayed intact for so long.

"On the pound" nicknames were appreciated and accepted since it was a step away from a man's birth name, or "government name," which was the name that all the corrections officers, administrative staff, and of course the courts, used when addressing convicts. So, on paper Jamel's name was Jamel

Ross. On paper, Jamel Ross was not considered to be a person, but a "convict" with the registration number 40949–054, something like the forty thousandth prisoner to be filtered through the Southern District of New York. The "054" being the sort of area code in his prison ID number. He was sentenced by Judge Benison in October of 1997, committed to eighty-four months—no parole, and three years probation. The conviction was for bank robbery. However, on appeal, the conviction was "adjusted" since there was no conclusive evidence that Jamel had a weapon. Nevertheless, Jamel certainly *did* have a weapon and fully intended to pull off a robbery, with a pen as his weapon. So, the time he was doing was more deserved than not.

But regardless of Jamel's level of involvement, it was suddenly very easy for him to share himself since he felt he had nothing to lose. It was much easier to speak to a reasonably attractive woman, as if there was good reasoning for the things he did and why. So, he went on explaining all of his dirty deeds to "Dr. Kay" Edmondson, as if this were a confessional where he'd be forgiven for his sins. And why not? She was a good-listening, career-oriented female. She was black and she wasn't condescending like so many other staff members were. And when she called him "Jamel," as opposed to "Convict Ross," it made him imagine they had a tighter bond in store.

"**So this dude**—I won't say his name—he let me in on his check game. He explained how one person could write a check for, say, one hundred grand, give it to a friend, and even if the money isn't there to back up the check, the depositor could likely withdraw money on it before it is found to be worthless. It sounded good. And I figured the worst case scenario would be to deny this and to deny that. . . ."

"They don't verify the check? I mean, isn't that like part of the procedure before it clears?" Kay generally did more talking than this when a convict sat before her. Except she was finding his story, as well as his in-depth knowledge of things, so fascinating.

"See, that's the thing. If the check comes from the same region, or if it's from the other side of the world, it still has to go through a clearing house, where all of the checks from *all* of the banks eventually go. So that takes like a couple of days. But banks—certain banks—are on some ol' 'we trust you' stuff, and I guess since they've got your name and address 'n' stuff, they do the cash within one or two days."

"Really?"

"Yup. They will if it's a local check from a local bank. And on that hundred grand? The bank will let loose on the second day. I'll go in and get the money when the dam breaks. . . ."

"And when the bank finds out about the check being no good?"

"I play dumb. I don't know the guy who wrote the check. Met him only twice, blah blah blah. I sign this little BS affidavit and *bang*—I'm knee-deep in free money."

Dr. Kay wagged her head of flowing hair and replied, "You all never cease to amaze me. I mean *you,* as in the convict here. I hear all sorts of tricks and shortcuts and—"

"Cons. They're cons, Doctor Kay."

"Sure, sure . . ." she somehow agreed.

"But it's all a dead-end, ya know? Like, once you get money, it becomes an addiction, to the point that you forget your *reasons* and *objectives* for getting money in the first place."

"Did *you* forget, Jamel?"

"Did I? I got *so deep* in the whole check thing that it became my new profession."

"Stop playin'."

"I'm for real. I started off with my own name and companies, but then, uhh . . ." Jamel hesitated. He looked away from the doctor. "I shouldn't really be tellin' you this. I'm ramblin'."

"You don't have to if you don't want to, but let me remind you that what you say to me in our sessions is confidential, unless I feel that you might cause harm to yourself or someone else, or if I'm subpoenaed to testify in court."

"Hmmm." Jamel deliberated on that. He wondered if the eighty-four month sentence could be enhanced to double or triple, or worse. He'd heard about the nightmares, how bragging while in prison was a tool that another prisoner could use to shorten his own sentence. "Informants" they called them. And just the *thought* of that made Jamel promise himself that he wouldn't say a thing about the weapon and the real reason he caught so much time.

"Off the record, Jamel . . ."

"Oooh, I like this 'off-the-record' stuff." Jamel rubbed his hands together and came to the edge of the couch from his slouched position.

"Well, to put your mind at ease, I haven't *yet* received a subpoena for a trial."

Jamel took that as an indication of secrecy and that he was supposed to have confidence in her. But he proceeded with caution as he went on explaining about the various bank scams, the phony licenses and bogus checks.

The doctor said, "Wow, Jamel. That's a hell of a switch. One day you're a television producer, a publisher, and a ladies man, and the next—"

The phone rang.

"I'm sorry." Dr. Kay got up from her chair, passed Jamel and circled her desk. It gave him a whiff of her perfume, and that only had him to pay special attention to her calves. There was something about a woman's calves that got him excited. Or didn't. But Dr. Kay's calves *did*. As she took her phone call, Jamel wondered if she did the StairMaster bit, or if she ran in the mornings. Maybe she was in the military like most of these prison guards claimed. Was she an aerobics instructor at some point in her life? All of those ideas were flowing like sweet Kool-Aid in Jamel's head as he thought and wondered and imagined.

"Could you excuse me?" Dr. Kay said.

"Sure," said Jamel, and he quickly stepped out of the office and shut the door behind him. Through the door's window he tried to cling to her words. It seemed to be a business call, but that was just a guess. A hope. It was part of Jamel's agenda to guess and wonder what this woman or that woman would be like underneath him, or on top of him. After all, he was locked up and unable to touch another being. So, his imaginings were what guided him during these seven years. He'd take time to look deep into a woman, and those thoughts weren't frivolous but anchored and supported by his past. Indeed, sex was a major part of his life from a teen. It had become a part of his lifestyle. Women. The fine ones. The ones who weren't so fine, but whom he felt he could "shape up and get right." Dr. Kay was somewhere in between those images. She had a cute face and an open attitude. Her eyes smiled large and compassionate. She was cheeky when she smiled, with lips wide and supple. Her teeth were bright and indicated good hygiene.

And Dr. Kay wasn't built like an *Essence* model or a dancer in a video. She was a little thick where it mattered, and she had what Jamel considered to be "a lot to work with."

Big-breasted with healthy hips, Dr. Kay was one of a half dozen women on the compound who were black. There were others who were Hispanic and a few more who were white. But of those who were somehow accessible, Dr. Kay nicely fit Jamel's reach. And to reach her, all he had to do was make the effort to trek on down to the psychology department, in the same building as the chapel and the hospital. All you had to do was express interest in counseling. Then you had to pass a litmus test of sorts, giving your reason for needing counseling. Of course, Dr. Kay wasn't the only psychotherapist in the department. There were one or two others. So Jamel had to hope and pray that his interview would 1) be with Dr. Kay Edmonson, and 2) that his address would be taken sincerely, not as just another sex-starved convict who wanted a whiff or an eyeful of the available female on the compound.

Considering all of that, Jamel played his cards right and was always able to have Dr. Kay set him up for a number of appointments. It couldn't be once a week; the doctor-convict relationship would quickly burn out at that rate. But twice a month was a good start, so that she could get a grip on who (and what) he was about. Plus, his visits wouldn't be so obvious as to raise any red flags with her boss, who, as far as Jamel could tell, really didn't execute any major checks and balances of Kay's caseload. Still, it was the other prisoners at Fort Dix who Jamel had to be concerned about. They had to be outsmarted at every twist and turn, since they were the very people (miserable, locked up, and jealous) who would often jump to conclusions. Anyone of these guys might get the notion, the hint, or the funny idea that Dr. Kay was getting too personal with one prisoner. Then the dime dropping and the investigation would begin.

HARLEM HEAT

By 50 Cent and Mark Anthony

Fast Forward to:
September 2006
Long Island, New York

I can't front. I was nervous as hell.

My heart was thumping a mile a minute, like it was about to jump outta my chest. The same goddamn state trooper had now been following us for more than three exits and I knew that it was just a matter of seconds before he was gonna turn on his lights and pull us over, so I put on my signal and switched lanes and prepared to exit the parkway, hoping that he would change his mind about stopping us.

"Chyna, what the fuck are you doing?" my moms asked me as she fidgeted in her seat.

"Ma, you know this nigga is gonna pull us over, so I'm just acting like I'm purposely exiting before he pulls us over. It'll be easier to play shit off if he does stop us."

"Chyna, I swear to God you gonna get us locked the fuck up. Just relax and drive!" my mother barked as she turned her head to look in the rearview mirror to confirm that the

rupting my words. He was clutching the nine-millimeter handgun, still in its holster, and he cautiously approached me. Soon, I no longer heard the music coming from the car and I was guessing that my mother had turned it down so that she could try and listen to what the officer was saying.

"Put my hands on the car for what? Let me just explain where I'm going."

The officer wasn't trying to hear it, and he slammed me up against the hood of the car.

"I got a sick baby in the car. What the hell is wrong with you?" I screamed. I was purposely trying to be dramatic while squirming my body and resisting the officer's efforts to pat me down.

On the inside I was still shitting bricks and my heart was still racing a mile a minute. The car was in park at the side of the road and the engine was running idle. I was hoping that my mom would jump into the driver's seat and speed the hell off. There was no sense in both of us getting bagged. And from the looks of things, the aggressive officer didn't seem like he was in the mood for bullshit.

"Is anyone else in the car with you?" the cop asked me as he felt between my legs up to my crotch, checking for a weapon—though he was clearly feeling for more than just a weapon.

My mother's 745 that I was driving had limousine-style tints, and the state trooper couldn't fully see inside the car.

"Just my moms and my sick baby. Yo, on the real, for real, this is crazy. I ain't even do shit and you got me bent over and

state trooper was still tailing us. She also reached to turn up the volume on the radio and then slumped in her seat a little bit, trying to relax.

Although my moms was trying to play shit cool, the truth was, I knew that she was just as nervous as I was.

"Ma, I already switched lanes, I gotta get off now or we'll look too suspicious," I explained over the loud R. Kelly and Snoop Dogg song that was coming from the speakers.

As soon as I switched lanes and attempted to make my way to the ramp of exit 13, the state trooper threw on his lights, signaling for me to pull over.

"Ain't this a bitch. Chyna, I told yo' ass."

"Ma, just chill," I barked, cutting my mother off. I was panicking and trying to think fast, and the last thing I needed was for my mother to be bitchin' with me.

"I got this. I'ma pull over and talk us outta this. Just follow my lead," I said with my heart pounding as I exited the parkway ramp and made my way on to Linden Boulevard before bringing the car to a complete stop.

I had my foot on the brake and both of my hands on the steering wheel. I inhaled deeply and then exhaled very visibly before putting the car in park. I quickly exited the car, still wearing my Cartier Aviator gold-rimmed shades to help mask my face. The loud R. Kelly chorus continued playing in the background.

"Officer, I'm sorry if I was speeding, but—"

"Miss, step away from the car and put your hands where I can see them," The lone state trooper shouted at me, inter-

slammed up against the hood of the car feeling all on my pussy and shit! I got a sick baby that I'm trying to get to the hospital," I yelled while trying to fast-talk the cop. I sucked my teeth and gave him a bunch of eye-rolling and neck-twisting ghetto attitude.

"You didn't do shit? Well if this is a BMW, then tell me why the fuck your plates are registered to a Honda Accord," the six-foot-four-inch drill-sergeant-looking officer screamed back at me.

The cop then reached to open up the driver's door, and just as he pulled the car door open, my moms opened her passenger door. She hadn't taken off the shades or the hat that she had been wearing, and with one foot on the ground and her other foot still inside the car she stood up and asked across the roof of the car if there was a problem.

"Chyna, you okay? What the fuck is going on, Officer?" my mother asked, sounding as if she was highly annoyed.

"Miss, I need you to step away from the car," the officer shouted at my mother.

"Step away from the car for what?" my moms yelled back with even more disgust in her voice.

"Ma, he on some bullshit, I told him that Nina is in the backseat sick as a damn dog and he still on this ol' racist profiling shit."

As soon as I was done saying those words I heard gunfire erupting.

Blaow. Blaow. Blaow. Blaow.

Instinctively I ducked for cover down near the wheel

well, next to the car's twenty-two-inch chrome rims. And when I turned and attempted to see where the shots were coming from, all I saw was the state trooper dropping to the ground. I turned and looked the other way and saw my mom's arms stretched across the roof of the BMW. She was holding her chrome thirty-eight revolver with both hands, ready to squeeze off some more rounds.

"Chyna, you aight?"

"Yeah, I'm good." I shouted back while still half-way crouched down near the tire.

"Well, get your ass in this car and let's bounce!" my moms screamed at me.

I got up off the ground from my kneeling stance and with my high-heeled Bottega Veneta boots I stepped over the bloody state trooper, who wasn't moving. He had been shot point-blank right between the eyes and he didn't look like he was breathing all that well, as blood spilled out of the side of his mouth.

Before I could fully get my ass planted on the cream-colored plush leather driver's seat my mom was hollering for me to hurry up and pull off.

"Drive this bitch, Chyna! I just shot a fucking cop! Drive!"

My mom's frantic yelling had scared my ten month-old baby, who was strapped in her carseat in the back. So with my moms screaming for me to hurry up and drive away from the crime scene and with my startled baby crying and hitting high notes I put the car in drive and I screeched off, leaving the lifeless cop lying dead in the street.

If shit wasn't thick enough for me and my mom already, killing a state trooper had definitely just made things a whole lot thicker. I sped off doing about sixty miles an hour down a quiet residential street in Elmont, Long Island, just off of Linden Boulevard. My heart was thumping and although it was late afternoon on a bright and sunny summer weekday, I was desperately hoping that no eyewitnesses had seen what went down.